Parrot in the Oven
mi vida

A novel by
Victor Martinez

Joanna Cotler Books

HarperTrophy®
A Division of HarperCollins*Publishers*

Parrot in the Oven
mi vida

Library of Congress Cataloging-in-Publication Data
Martinez, Victor, date
    Parrot in the oven : mi vida / a novel by Victor Martinez.
        p.   cm.
    "Joanna Cotler books."
    Summary: Manny relates his coming of age experiences as a
member of a poor Mexican family in which the alcoholic father
only adds to everyone's struggle.
    ISBN 0-06-026704-6. — ISBN 0-06-026706-2 (lib. bdg.)
    ISBN 0-06-447186-1 (pbk.)
    [1. Family life—Fiction.   2. Alcoholism—Fiction.
3. Mexican Americans—Fiction.]   I. Title.
PZ7.M36718Par 1996   96-2119
[Fic]—dc20   CIP
                                                          AC

Typography by Steve Scott
    OPM   20   19   18

❖

First Harper Trophy edition, 1998

Visit us on the World Wide Web!
http://www.harperchildrens.com

To my mother, Olivia,
and my father, Victor

contents

■1■

The Baseball Glove

That summer my brother, Bernardo, or "Nardo," as we call him, flipped through more jobs than a thumb through a deck of cards. First he was a dishwasher, then a busboy, then a parking attendant and, finally, a patty turner for some guy who never seemed to be in his hamburger stand for more than ten minutes at a time. (Mom believed he sold marijuana, or did some other illegal shamelessness.) Nardo lost one job for not showing up regular enough, another for showing up too regular—the boss hated his guts. The last job lost him when the owner of the hamburger stand packed up unexpectedly and left for Canada.

The job Nardo misses most, though, was when he worked as a busboy for the Bonneville Lakes Golf and Catering Service. He says it was the only time he ever got to touch elbows with rich people. The parties they catered served free daiquiris, whisky drinks and cold beer, really cold, in big barrels choking with ice. At some parties, like the

1

one he got fired from, they passed out tickets for juicy prizes like motorcycles, TV sets, stereos and snow skis. The last party had a six-piece band and a great huge dance floor so the "old fogies," as my brother called them, could get sloshed and make fools of themselves.

As it turns out, he and a white guy named Randy took off their busboy jackets and began daring each other to get a ticket and ask a girl to dance. Randy bet Nardo wouldn't do it, and Nardo bet he would, and after a two-dollar pledge he steered for the ticket lady.

"I could've hashed it around a bit, you know, Manny," he said. "I could've double- and triple-dared the guy a couple of times over, then come up with a good excuse. But that ain't my style."

Instead he tapped Randy's fingers smooth as fur and walked up to the ticket lady. She peered out from behind the large butcher-paper-covered table at the blotches of pasta sauce on his black uniform pants and white shirt—which were supposed to go clean with the catering service's light-orange busboy jacket, but didn't—and said, "Ah, what the hell," and tore him out a tag.

Before the little voice nagging inside him could talk louder, Nardo asked the nearest girl for

2

a dance. She had about a million freckles and enough wire in her mouth to run a toy train over. They stumbled around the dance floor until the band mercifully ground to a halt. She looked down at his arm kind of shylike and said, "You dance real nice."

Now my brother had what you could call a sixth sense. *"Es muy vivo,"* as my grandma used to say about a kid born that way, and with Nardo it was pretty much a scary truth. He could duck trouble better than a champion boxer could duck a right cross. He made hairline escapes from baths, belt whippings and scoldings just by not being around when punishment came through the door. So I believed him when he said something ticklish crawled over his shoulder, and when he turned around, there, across the dance floor, in front of the bandleader about to make an announcement over the microphone, was his boss, Mr. Baxter—and boy was he steamed!

Mr. Baxter owned the catering service, and sometimes, my brother said, the way he'd yell at the busboys, it was like he owned them, too. Mr. Baxter didn't say anything, just pointed to the door, then at Nardo, and scratched a big X across his chest. Just like that, he was fired.

3

The way Nardo tells it, you'd think he did that man a favor working for him. "Don't you ever get braces, Manny," he said, as if that were the lesson he'd learned.

At first Nardo didn't want to go to the fields. Not because of pride, although he'd have used that excuse at the beginning if he could've gotten away with it. It was more because, like anyone else, he didn't like sobbing out tears of sweat in 110-degree sun. That summer was a scorcher, maybe the worst in all the years we'd lived in that valley desert, which our town would've been if the irrigation pumped in from the Sierra were turned off. I could tell how searing it was by the dragged-out way my mom's roses drooped every morning after I watered them. The water didn't catch hold. The roses only sighed a moment before the sun sucked even that little breather away.

Although it was hard for Nardo to duck my mom's accusing eyes, especially when Magda, my sister, came home slumped from the laundry after feeding bedsheets all day into a steam press, he was refusing to work anymore. Whether one tried threats, scoldings, or even shaming, which my mom tried almost every other day,

4

nothing worked. We all gave it a shot, but none more vigorously than my dad. He'd yell and stomp around a little space of anger he'd cut in our living room, a branch of spit dangling from his lip. He'd declare to the walls what a good-for-nothing son he had, even dare Nardo to at least be man enough to join the Army. He vowed to sign the papers himself, since Nardo wasn't old enough.

The thing was, my dad wasn't working either. He'd just lost his job as a translator for the city because he'd drink beer during lunch and slur his words. Ever since losing his job, and even before, really, Dad had about as much patience as you could prop on a toothpick. He was always zeroing in on things he wanted to be disappointed in, and when he found one, he'd loose a curse quicker than an eyeblink. Even when he wasn't cursing, you could still feel one simmering there under his lip, ready to boil over.

Even though he'd worked as a translator, my dad's English wasn't the greatest. Some syllables he just couldn't catch. Instead of saying "watch," he'd say "wash," and for "stupid," he'd slip in a bit of Spanish, "*es*-tupid." But when he said "ass" or "ounce," stretching the S with a long,

5

lingering slowness, there was pure acid in the set of his teeth.

"If only Bernardo had jus whuan ounss, whuan ounss . . ." my dad would say, making the tiniest measure between his thumb and forefinger, but with a voice the size of our whole block.

For his part, Nardo stayed home lifting weights and doing sit-ups and push-ups, and nursing any piddling little pimple worth a few hours of panic. He was a nut about his handsome looks, and must have tenderly combed his hair at least twenty times a day in the mirror.

I wasn't like Nardo. I suppose years of not knowing what, besides work, was expected from a Mexican convinced me that I wouldn't pass from this earth without putting in a lot of days. I suppose Nardo figured the same, and wasn't about to waste his time. But I was of my grandpa Ignacio's line of useful blood. All his life, no matter what the job, my grandpa worked like a man trying to fill all his tomorrows with one solid day's work. Even in the end, when he got sick and couldn't move, he hated sitting on the couch doing nothing. He'd fumble around the house fixing sockets and floor trim, painting lower shelves and screwing legs back on to tables, although the finished chore was always more a sign of how much his mind had gotten older than anything else.

For a while, I hustled fruit with my cousins Rio and Pete. Their dad, my uncle Joe, owned a panel truck, and together we sold melons, apples, oranges—whatever grew in season—from door to door. But when my uncle hurt his leg tripping over some tree roots, and his ankle swelled up blue and tender as a ripened plum and he couldn't walk, except maybe to hobble on one leg to the refrigerator or lean over to change channels on the TV, he took the panel truck away.

Without work, I was empty as a Coke bottle. School was starting soon, and I needed money for clothes and paper stuff. I wanted a baseball mitt so bad a sweet hurt blossomed in my stomach whenever I thought about it. Baseball had a grip on my fantasies then, and I couldn't shake it loose. There was an outfielder's glove in the window of Duran's Department Store that kept me dreaming downright dangerous outfield catches. I decided to stir up Nardo to see if he'd go pick chili peppers with me.

"You can buy more weights!" I said a bit too enthusiastically, making him suspicious right off the bat.

He looked up at me from the middle of a push-up. "You think I'm lazy, don't you?"

"No," I lied.

"Yeah, you do. You think I'm lazy," he said, breathing tight as he pushed off the floor.

"I said no!"

"Yeah, you do." He forced air into his lungs, then got up miserably wiping his hands.

"But that's all right, little boy, if you think I'm lazy. Everybody else does." He started picking at a sliver in his palm. "I'm not really lazy, you know. I've been working off and on." He greedily bit the sliver, moving his elbow up and down like a bird's wing. "If Mom wants me to go," he said, finally, "I'll go. If that's what *she* wants. But I'm telling you right now, if it gets hot I'm quitting."

Miracles don't wait for doubters, so the next morning I asked my dad if we could borrow his car, a Plymouth, which Nardo could drive despite the tricky gearshift. Dad was pretty cheery about me getting Nardo out of hibernation. He gave us some paint cans for the chili peppers and practically put a Christmas ribbon on the large brimmed hats from Mexico he'd bought years ago. The headbands were already dark with sweat and the straw furry with dust, but they'd protect us from the sun.

When we arrived at the chili field, the wind through the window was warm on our shirt-sleeves. Already the sky was beginning to hollow out, the clouds rushing toward the rim of the horizon as if even they knew the sun would soon be the center of a boiling pot.

The foreman, wearing a pale-yellow shirt with a black-leather vest and cowboy boots with curled tips, refused at first to hire us, saying I was too young, that it was too late in the day—most field workers got up at the first wink of dawn. Besides, all the rows had been taken hours ago. He laughed at the huge lunch bag bulging under Nardo's arm, and said we looked like two kids strolling out on a picnic.

Although he could fake disappointment better than anybody, deep down I believed Nardo wanted to give picking chilies a try. But a good excuse was a good excuse, and any excuse was better than quitting. So he hurriedly threw his can into the car trunk and made a stagy flourish with his hand before opening the side door.

Seeing him so spunky, I thought it nothing less than torture when the foreman said that,

9

fortunately for us, there was a scrawny row next to the road no one wanted. The foreman must have thought it a big joke, giving us that row. He chuckled and called us over with a sneaky offer of his arm, as if to share a secret.

"Vamos, muchachos, aquí hay un surco muy bueno que pueden piscar," he said, gesturing down at some limp branches leaning away from the road, as if trying to lift their roots and hustle away from the passing traffic. The leaves were sparse and shriveled, dying for air, and they had a coat of white pesticide dust and exhaust fumes so thick you could smear your hands on the leaves and rub fingerprints with them.

My brother shrugged. His luck gone, there was not much else he could do. The foreman hung around a bit to make sure we knew which peppers to pick and which to leave for the next growing, not that it mattered in that row.

We'd been picking about two hours when the sun began scalding the backs of our hands, leaving a pocket of heat crawling like a small animal inside our shirts. My fingers were as rubbery as old carrots, and it seemed forever before the peppers rose to the center of my can. Nardo topped his can before I did, patted the chilies down and lifted it over his shoulder, his rock of an arm solid against his cheek.

"I'm gonna get my money and buy me a soda," he said, and strode off toward the weighing area, carefully swishing his legs between the plants. I limped behind him, straining with my half-filled can of lungless chili peppers.

The weighing area wasn't anything special, just a tripod with a scale hook hanging from the center. People brought their cans and sagging burlap sacks and formed a line. After the scale pointer flipped and settled, heaving with the sack's weight, the peppers were dumped onto a wooden table-bed. Tiny slits between the boards let the mixed-in dirt and leaves sift through.

There was a line of older women and young girls with handkerchiefs across their faces. They stood along the sides, like train robbers in cowboy movies, cleaning the leaves and clods of dirt, pushing the peppers down through a chute. When the sack at the end bloated, one of the foremen unhooked it from the nails and sewed the opening. Then he stacked it on a pile near a waiting truck whose driver lay asleep in the cab with boots sticking out in the blurry currents of air.

Standing near the table-bed, my eyes flared

and nose dribbled a mustache of watery snot. The dried leaves and the angry scent of freshly broken peppers was like being swarmed by bees. No matter how hard I tried to keep my breath even, I kept coughing and choking like I had a crushed ball of sandpaper stuffed in my throat. I wondered how the women were able to stand it, even with the handkerchiefs.

The only good thing about the weighing area was that they paid right after announcing your load. This lured workers from Mexico needing quick cash for rent or emergency food, and people like me who had important baseball mitts to buy. It also brought business to a burrito truck behind the scales owned by the labor contractor. It sold everything from chicken tacos, chili beans and egg burritos, to snow cones and fudge bars.

The prices, though, made Nardo complain real loud: "You know how much I paid for this!" he exclaimed, when out of earshot of the foreman. "Eighty-five cents! Eighty-five cents for a damn soda! And to top it off, it's one of those cheap jobs with no fizzle or nothing."

We picked steadily on, but by noon both Nardo and I were burned out, with our tongues flagging in the heat, and a good sprint away from the nearest picker. Farther up, under clouds boiling like water on the horizon, a staggered string of men worked two and three rows apiece.

"They're wetbacks," my brother explained; "they pick like their goddamned lives depended on it."

I looked over at the Mexican man working on the rows next to ours and nodded agreement. He handled four rows all by himself, using two cans, and trading handfuls from one can to the other. He'd go up two rows, then down two rows, greeting us on his return with a smile and shy wave. To save time, he placed burlap sacks every twenty feet, and every half hour or so he'd pour a loaded can into the closest. Behind him, three sacks already lay fat and tightly sewn. We eyed him, amazed by his quickness.

"Maybe that's what we should do," I suggested.

Nardo shook his head. "Are you crazy?" he asked with conviction. "It'll take us the whole damn day just to fill one lousy sack."

He was right. We weren't the best pickers in the field; we weren't even close to being the worst. We stopped too much, my brother to eye the girls near the weigher, and me to watch the man and compare hands. His were wings in a blur of wonder, mine stirred a pot of warm honey. The way he moved, too, made me think he'd make a terrific shortstop, what with the way he shifted from plant to plant, his knees like a triangle, tilting first one way then another. He was a whirlwind when gathering up his cans and burlap sacks, and eyeing him this way, with admiration, almost made me forget my own tiredness, although he never seemed to tire, never seemed to rise much above the plant, but hid inside the quivering leaves until with one flickering toss, a rain of yellow peppers showered the air and dropped into his can.

I was marveling at him when Nardo tapped me on the shoulder. "Look what's coming," he said, pointing his chin at a van creeping up the road.

Cars had been insulting us with dust and exhaust fumes all morning, so when I saw how this van approached, like a dog sneaking up on a bush, I knew something was wrong.

The van was green, a dim, starved-for-light green, like the leaves on our row. Its windows were open and the man behind the wheel had his head out scanning the rows. Suddenly people began to stand up, licking the air and stretching as if peering over a high wall. There was fast talking in Spanish and frenzied commotion as suddenly forty or so people all at once jumped up and started running. They didn't even bother going through the furrows in scissor steps like Nardo had done, but ran in waves, trampling over plants and tipping over cans. Those last to run brought up the rear, steadying their hats with one hand and thrashing their snapped-up coats in the other.

I still didn't know what was going on. My first thought was to run, but when I saw three more vans and a large labor bus pop out of a narrow road in the cornfield bordering ours, I knew that Immigration had come for the people.

No one had seen the other vans place themselves at points along the cornfield. The people just ran wildly in panic toward them as if their first thought was to hide in the stalks. The quicker ones got caught at once, their paths cut off by officers holding out their arms. They surrendered without a word. The slower ones veered off into the open spaces of the cordon and dove into the field. Most were caught in the first sweep, except for some who ducked under the arms of the officers and hustled down the road; but they, too, were quickly run down by another van and escorted inside.

The handful who hid in the cornstalks seemed to have gotten away. We all cheered and waved our arms as if our side had won. Some of us jeered at the officers, my brother Nardo the loudest.

Everyone quieted down, though, when some of the officers formed a line along the field and disappeared into the stalks. A while later they came out yanking on the shirt collars of those we thought had gotten away. Everybody sighed and said nothing.

The foreman who'd given us the scraggly row rushed over to see what was going on. He took off in a huff saying "son-ova-beeches," and worse. I thought he was going to cuss those Immigration guys off, but instead he stood by meekly watching the officers corral the people before loading them into the vans. I tried to find the Mexican on the row next to ours, but I didn't see him. I hoped he'd gotten away.

The officer in charge approached the foreman and said something we couldn't make out, but it sounded like a scolding. The foreman came back and knelt down by the water tank. "Damn son-ova-beeches," he said again, flicking his hat off and raising dust as he slapped it against his pant leg. He poured himself some water and glared over at the Immigration officers as they packed in the people and roared off in a boiling cloud of dust. A crowd of us stood around covering our eyes. No one bothered to go back to work.

When the air cleared, a man tottered back from the spot where the vans had assembled. He was an older man with salt-and-pepper stubble on his chin and a slightly longer and darker mustache. He was nursing his right knee.

At first I thought maybe he'd gotten away, but then someone recognized him and laughed, "Hey Joe, you're not a wetback. You're a *bracero*."

Joe came slowly over and took off his hat and covered his stomach as if he'd been caught naked. He shrugged an apology and said he couldn't help it, when everyone else began to run, he got so excited he ran too. He looked down at his legs as if they'd betrayed him. He said Immigration let him go as soon as they saw he had too much meat on his bones to be a wetback. Everybody laughed. Then his family, whose confused uncle he was, came over and led him away. Nardo and I laughed too, but for some reason I thought he was the best man in the whole field.

Of the twenty or so people left, everyone

claimed they encouraged the Mexicans not to run. They said Immigration guys usually don't go into the fields to check for citizenship unless they have a good reason. If you acted like you belonged, sometimes you could fool them. They said none of those ungratefuls took them at their word, though, and for that they had only themselves to blame.

One of the listeners, a tall pimple-faced guy with blotchy cheeks and the skin of a fig, only paler, shouted out, "*Pinches gavachos* don't give a damn about harassing us! *Gavachos* do what they want." He didn't wait for anybody to answer back, nor did he pick up any cans or equipment, but walked quickly away, swung open the door of a rusty Buick and drove off.

"I guess he came alone," Nardo said musingly. He rubbed his eyes with the backs of his wrists, then became more alert. "Hey, we can pick on any row we want now."

"That man's crazy! Those people don't live here, anyway," said a short, moist-faced guy with tight bunched-in cheeks and pants that settled unevenly around his waist. When he walked, one of his legs looked shorter than the other. He went over to one of the rows a Mexican had been picking on and lifted up a pair of old shoes. The soles were crusted with mud and the leather scarred and furrowed like the faces of old men who've worked in the fields all their lives. He held them at the tips of his fingers and away from his precious nose. The man who wore them probably had taken them off in the heat to stick his toes in the moist, irrigated soil. A small chorus of laughter went up when he held them high, then fell when he dropped them back to earth. He rummaged some more down the row until he found a sack bulging with chili peppers.

"Hey, I'm gonna keep these," he declared, and began dragging the sack.

When everyone saw this they all began to scramble around for the other abandoned sacks, claiming their right by how close their rows had been to the Mexicans beside them. The sacks belonging to the man working on the rows next to ours were laying, tightly sewn, on their sides. Nardo walked over and placed his hand on one. Two other guys came over to argue about whom the others belonged to, but my brother was stronger, and after some half-serious pushing and shoving they walked away grumbling.

"Look, Manny," Nardo said, excitedly spearing up his shirtsleeves. He lifted one sack by its ears and pounded it on the ground, packing the peppers down its belly. "We got more here than it'd take us two days to pick. Hey, you can even buy your mitt."

I thought of the baseball glove, all clean and stiff and leather-smelling, and of myself in the cool green lawn of center field. I imagined already being on the baseball team at school, and people looking at me. Not these people picking chilies or those sent away in the vans, but people I had yet to know, watching me as I stood mightily in center field. I looked down at the sacks, then far out in the distance at the clouds of dust folding and unfolding where the vans were pulling away. I wondered how long I'd have had to work to fill those sacks. The weariness of it stretched as wide as the horizon.

■ 2 ■

Rico's Pool Hall

ico's Pool Hall was Dad's favorite spot in the whole world. Among four pool tables made of solid wood, cobwebs of smoke drifting to the ceiling, the air smelling hearty of varnished wood, field sweat, beer and farts, he breathed easy. All day he talked to his buddies about Mexico, and about schemes for making money and escaping back to Mexico—although some of the men there were born in the United States.

Kids weren't allowed in the pool hall, but Rico let me stay sometimes while waiting for Dad. I'd sit on a stool at the far end of the bar, watching guys lean against pool cues, smoke and cuss one another out. I even saw a fight once where a guy threw a cue ball at a man in a Texas hat and smacked his teeth clean off the gums.

Because of his drinking, and because of the milk she said drained into the gutter whenever he drank, Mom hated to see Dad go to Rico's. She was always dragging me along with her to bring him home. On the day after the chili peppers, we were all piled in the car—my little sister Pedi whining about the heat, Magda clapping her hands to the rock-and-roll music inside her head, Dad complaining about a streak of clever pool shots he was working on before Mom yanked him rudely away. No telling how much money he could have won, he kept saying.

Steam puffed from my mouth and my nose ached from the heavy tar smell of melting asphalt. That's when I did a stupid thing. I put my arm on the car door and shouted, "Dammit!" as I jerked from the searing metal.

Sitting in the front seat, Mom heard me, and before I could plead excuses, she reached over her shoulder and smacked me one on the mouth. There were certain rules that needed no part of a brain's labor for Mom to smack me one. If she caught me cursing, or breaking a glass, she'd pound my arm. Twice if the curse had anything to do with girls, or the glass had milk. Also, whatever gossip could cling to our family for as long as people's memories lasted, I was to avoid.

With my Dad, it was more simple. If I grew a bit too raucous, he'd put a vise grip on my shoulder and whisper hot breath inside my ear.

"Settle down quick, Manuel," he'd say, "or elsse."

Luckily, he was still too soaked from drinking at the pool hall to pay me any mind. He did get into it with the three Garcia brothers, though, who were lazying around their front yard.

"¡Qué chingados!" he exclaimed, as we drove into the parking lot. "Those bastards, drinking beer and laughing out of their mouths. They'd suck their mother's last milk if she wasn't dead."

Dad was angry at the Garcias for destroying his dream. He had bought this croquet set, with which he planned to play with the neighbors while lounging away the hot afternoons. But on the first day we brought it home, the Garcias came over like wild chimpanzees. Bobby wrestled a mallet out of my hands and tossed it into a tree, and Stinky stole a wire wicket while Dad's back was turned. Dad vowed never again to favor our neighborhood with culture.

I slunk my chin low while Dad slowed the car and gazed acidly at the Garcias. They pretended these big, idiot smiles, and seeing them act so disrespectful, Dad yelled out the window, "Where're your girlfriends. Did you send them off to work for you?"

This riled Bobby and Stinky, who were old

23

enough to have girlfriends but didn't. They started pushing their chairs around searching for a rock, but Dad laughed and pumped the gas.

He was chuckling under his breath when he pulled up in front of our house, made of Sheetrock and a gravel-tile roof. Shaped like box hotels in a Monopoly set, the houses weren't pretty or stylish, but in spring the grass flowed to every porch like green water lapping against the hulls of houseboats, and that was beautiful. But now it was summer, and the heat had sucked the grass blond.

Dad seemed to like his clever joke, so I figured the next best thing for him was to start in about the Welfare, and sure enough, he fired his two cents into that one. Actually, Mom started him off, so I shouldn't blame Dad, totally. She mentioned how some men from the projects were earning money from jobs the Welfare gave them. She'd seen them coming home with metal lunch pails and shirts flagging out of their pants.

"But you know how the Welfare is," Dad said. "They want to know everything. A social worker comes over, acting like we're criminals. Then the whole neighborhood knows we're getting Welfare."

He looked dazed, Dad did, like if you tapped

him on the shoulder he'd bolt off running down the street. Mom just pursed her lips. She knew he was just groping for something to complain about. Besides, half of the projects were already getting Welfare, and the other half were trying to get on. This didn't stop Dad, though.

"They'll make a copy of my driver's license, Rebecca," he insisted, "and it will stay in their files." After grinding his finger about fifty times in the air, he added, "Besides, I have never done anything in my whole life that would make me beg."

"Would you rather let the kids starve?" Mom asked, indignant and, as usual, making a ton of sense.

This reddened Dad's face more than the beer had already, but even he knew those canned meats and yellow bricks of butter the Welfare gave away wouldn't be half bad.

But it was no use. Dad believed weasely guys already owned the world, and anything you could do to get over on them was useless. He believed people were like money. If you were a million-dollar person, you had a grip on things, a big house maybe, and a crowd of suckers you could push around. You could be a thousand-dollar person or a hundred-dollar person—even a ten-,

25

five-, or one-dollar person. Below that, everybody was just nickels and dimes. To my dad, we were pennies.

Finally, he slowed down the wheels in his brain. "I'll get a job," he said, sullenly, "don't worry about it, I'll get job." Then he got out of the car and rushed inside, slinking through the hydraulic screen door.

Mom just gazed at the empty space where he had disappeared, then smirked her lips away from her teeth. She'd heard it all before. Ever since he lost his job with the city, every day he'd zoom on about the Welfare, or about the Garcias, or how he was going to get another job, this time on a higher floor.

I always wondered why he got so tossed around by things, why he'd roughen his voice and tire himself out complaining. Mom was more quiet. Whenever she worried about something, she'd bite her nails and look up at the sky; not like she was staring at the clouds, but like the whole sky was the most marvelous sight she'd ever seen.

When they started shouting and throwing their arms around, which I knew they'd do as soon as Mom walked in through the door, it was best to disappear. Even the walls sweated. Mom's shrieks chased away the panicked air; Dad's voice was coarse paper shredding to pieces. Sometimes I'd climb the elm tree out back or race over to my friend Frankie's, where the TV talked all day with nobody listening.

As I left, I saw my sister Magda through the window listening to records. She was singing to herself, stabbing her hands in the air like a belly dancer. "Everything's awright. Everything's gonna be awright," she sang.

I speeded across the parking lot, my eyelids heavy under the sun, grumbling over my mom's criminal unfairness. My lip was pulsing from where she had slapped me, and a swatch of blood smeared when I dabbed it with my fingers. My steps were snapping crisply on the dry shoots of blond grass when I reached the Big Lawn, where almost all year round the guys in our projects either smacked a baseball around or ran football plays, while our mothers, on plastic chairs, visited with one another, drinking iced tea and sprinkling gossip on the backs of those who got up to do chores.

Suddenly a dog crashed out of some side bushes, grunting and hunkering low, froth blowing from his mouth. I was afraid he was

27

coming to clamp his jaws on my leg, but then I saw the Garcia brothers, Bobby, Stinky and Little Tommy, chasing him with sticks. Stinky let fly a rock and it whizzed past my ear. Whether he was aiming at the dog or me, I wasn't sure, but they sure weren't going to catch the dog. Its paws were practically blistering on the asphalt.

The Garcias slowed down to a trot and veered toward me. Stinky, who was sweating enough to drip drops on the ground, was wearing a dingy gray T-shirt and jeans that looked as if they'd been scraped with rocks. Little Tommy had on a yellow-plaid shirt. Bobby wore a long green Pendleton shirt with red and gold patterns. His arms were straight at his sides, like he didn't want to wrinkle anything, and his mouth crooked funny when his head tilted back.

"Hey, it's the Hernandez boy," Bobby said over his shoulder to his brothers. Then, turning to me, he said, "Hey, Hernandez, I hear your fawder's got a job in the Welfare?"

I didn't bother denying it. Nothing anybody said could sink in with the Garcias.

"Hey, Manny." This time it was Stinky, twisting a stick in his hand, acting like he'd just thought up something terrific. He was in my grade at school, but about three years older than everybody else. He had ratty shoulders and two large can-opener teeth. His black hair was swatted smooth with pomade, and his voice sounded like two knife blades rubbing together.

I'd always been afraid of him. Every year at school he made it a habit of punching me around to show he was still boss. Once he broke a bone in my little finger, and I lied to Mom about it, saying that I got it sliding into second base. Another time he separated the soft rubber on the bridge of my nose, and I had to tell her I got hit by a pop fly.

Stinky was either hitching up his pants or trying to pull a knife out of his back pocket, I couldn't tell. "Where're *your* girlfriends, huh, Manny? You got any girls on you?"

Bobby, the oldest, came over and slung a lazy arm over my shoulder. I thought maybe he wanted to give my head a knuckle burn, but instead he looked into my ear as if peering into a microscope. He started fiddling with the collar of my shirt, twisting it like a necklace around his finger. His breath smelled gamy, of beer and sour pork. "You think your dad could get us some girls, Manny?" he said. "Your Dad knows a lot about that, huh?" He pulled on my collar. "What-aya say, Manny?"

Then he yanked hard again on my collar. I jerked back for balance but slipped and smashed my hip against the sidewalk. I stood up in an eye-blink, not wanting to be lying there with the Garcias around. Inside me something knotted, began to gel, then jiggle, as if shaking loose from under a trembling light. Even Little Tommy could tell I was scared. He was bouncing up and down, his scrawny legs working furiously, his fists clenched above his ears.

Stinky shoved his way back in and pressed his palm against my chest. "Hey, Manny," he said, "why don't you fix me a date with your sister, *ése*?"

"She doesn't go on dates," I said, but right away knew that I'd made a mistake by talking.

"Oh yeah, why don't she go on dates, huh?" Stinky asked. "What? Does she think she's too good for me? Is that it, *ése*? Is she too good for me now?" Stinky's fist was wound tight and he was jabbing it close to my face. I could see little white lightning bolts between his knuckles.

"My dad says she's too young."

"Too young!" Stinky exploded, fanning open

his fingers. He started flinching his arms. "Man, she must be nineteen or something!"

Then Little Tommy, looking ornery and offended, huffed over and planted his bony chest against mine. He had a big smudge of dirt on his cheek and a glob of gum stuck in his uncombed hair. He glared at me with his tiny anger, but Stinky wasn't finished, and again elbowed his way between us.

"Who in the hell does your sister think she is anyways . . . the Queen of Sheba? I oughta kick your frickin' ass right here, just ta show you no one's too good for me." He slowly cranked back his fist as if to clobber me, but then Bobby, who looked sleepy, like someone had poured Karo syrup over his face, shoved him away.

"Get back, Stinky! He's just a punk."

"Hey, it's Manny who *wants* to fight, not me," Stinky exclaimed, exaggerating his voice. "Look Bobby, he's *making* a fist at me!" When Bobby turned, Stinky steered around him and flung a blow at my chin, his fingers whiffing the air near my nose. "Hey, you wanna fight?" he said, stepping back and shuffling his feet around like a boxer admiring his moves.

Stinky was wild about himself. He began

31

clowning around, winding his arms and bluffing blows at my face. "I'll break your nose again, boy," he said, snapping his fingers. "I'll make that bump on your nose bigger. You'll lose ten pounds just taking in my punches."

Pushing Stinky away, Bobby turned to me with a creamy voice. "Whatsa matter with you, Manny, don't you *like* us?"

Just like that, they lost interest in me, and started walking across the Big Lawn toward the Yellow Projects. A cold ache of fear thawed in my chest, but I didn't move, thinking that if I did, they'd reel around and start bullying me again. When they were a little farther away, Stinky turned around, waving at me like I was his best friend in the whole world—which, actually, even after all the times he beat me up, I really think he believed.

"Next time, Aw'm gonna kick your ass!" he said, smiling friendly.

I decided to head back home. I didn't want to risk running into them again. The sky was scarred with clouds shaped like giant hoof marks, but the sun was hot and sputtering on the rim of the horizon. It was like walking into an ocean of heat.

When I got home, everything was quiet. I saw

Magda through the window of her room, cleaning bits of dust from her records. On the porch, Pedi was playing jacks with a golf ball Nardo had stolen from Bonneville Lakes Golf and Catering. I tousled her hair and stepped inside.

Dad was sitting on the living-room couch, his feet propped on the coffee table, drinking a can of beer and nipping little gulps of tequila from a pint bottle. In the kitchen, Mom was scrubbing the counter. She had her black hair braided into a solid coil in the back and was wearing a flower-print apron with the sleeves puffed like biscuits.

Mom was wild about daytime movies. When the music on the TV quickened, she'd angle her head through the doorway and watch the action. When there was a lot of talking, she'd scrub hard on the daisy-print linoleum. I thought she was going to grab me by the collar and plant me in front of the sink to wash dishes; instead, she said, "*Mijo*, you're blocking the TV!"

"What are you watching?"

"A Tony Curtis movie."

Standing behind a liquor bar, Tony was rustling ice cubes in a glass and twirling a spoon in suave, romantic circles. He glinted his eyes enticingly at some jazzy-looking blond lady—Marilyn Monroe, or somebody—lounging on a billowy couch. The blond lady didn't suspect a thing. Or maybe she did. Mom sure in the hell did. She knew Tony.

While I was standing there watching the off-and-on squiggles on the TV, Mom grabbed me by the shoulder and shoved me aside. "Move, *mijo*!" she said, craning her neck.

Although sitting close to the TV, Dad was pretending like he wasn't watching. He'd get interested in the parts where Mom's eyes glued on Tony, though. He'd stretch his leg across the coffee table to block out part of the screen, knowing this annoyed her, although she was trying hard to ignore him.

After a while, Mom came into the living room like gravity was pulling at her. She sat on the arm of the couch and propped her chin on her palms. So close was Tony to the blond lady that you could practically zipper their eyelashes together.

That's when Dad got up, snatching angrily at the air, and huffed into the bathroom. He washed, slapped on aftershave and smoothed his hair back with Red Rose brilliantine. He came out wearing a white shirt and black pants, like he was dressing for a funeral. Fat chance he was going to stick around to watch Tony smooch with the blond lady,

while Mom swooned. He was heading back to
Rico's to see if he could connect again with his
lucky shooting streak. He stood over Mom for
about a minute to see if she'd lift her eyes, then
grinned meanly, grabbed his keys and pint of
tequila and stormed out.

Mom just kept watching the TV. I guess she
figured she could scold him for starving us, scold
him about the unpaid rent or the job somewhere
in the world waiting for him to try harder, but she
was tired of all that. She knew if she cluttered his
ears with too much griping, it would only thicken
his stubbornness. He'd smolder around the house
for hours, grumbling and haranguing until he
gnawed her patience down to shreds.

Outside, I heard the car starter winding, but
it wouldn't kick over. "God dammit!" Dad shouted.

I pushed the curtains back and saw him
wrestling with the arm of the gear shift, which
sometimes stuck. He slammed his feet on the
floor and shook the wheel; then, relaxing his
hands, he stared hard at me, like I was weeds
growing wild in a field that some day he'd have
to chop.

Mom came up behind me and pressed down
on my shoulders, her hands smelling of ammonia.

We watched as Dad got out of the car and walked across the parking lot, grumbling. The hoof-mark clouds in the sky had burned away, and already I could see the wind beginning to smooth out the wrinkles of the afternoon heat. Pedi was still on porch, erasing some sparrows tracks on the dusty concrete.

Two of the Garcia brothers, Bobby and Stinky, snuck out from behind our neighbor Sophie's house and followed Dad, laughing and shoving each other with dares. They threw little pieces of gravel at him, trying to land them inside his neck collar, but he only swiped at the air behind his head and kept walking.

I turned around and saw the thick cords on Mom's neck, pulsing. She looked at me, and with a funny smile squeezed her fingers against my cheeks, sparking tiny needles of pain. When she let go, my face stung with a glowing warmth.

▪3▪

Charity

The next day, Mom began thinking about the future. She wanted me to go to a better school across town, where all the white kids got educated. So I grabbed the number 42 bus down Chandler Avenue, walked two blocks to the brown, ivy-rusted walls of my high school, and presented a note from my mom to Mrs. Kingsley, the secretary. Mom had heard rumors that they didn't like kids leaving my school and sometimes would mix things up for months, so she wanted me to get a record of my grades in person.

Mrs. Kingsley was an old white lady with cat-eye glasses dangling on a silver chain necklace. She had a pasty face, thick berry-painted lips and enough wrinkles on her neck to make a parachute. After giving her the note—she seemed to know what it was about, but asked me to read it anyway, I guess to test my English—she slid out a manila folder from a squeaky steel cabinet and, with an "I know more than you" smile, handed me the records. Her eyes casually dropped along the length of my arm, and just as I was about to grab the folder, she pushed it away like a worm had plopped down on it from the ceiling.

While waiting to catch the bus, I thought about calling Dad to see if he'd give me a ride home, but figured he was still numb from drinking the night before and would probably scold me for the hell of it. Besides, Mom wanted to keep it hush about me attending a school across town. She thought schooling could graduate me into places that would make her eyes gleam. Dad thought I should cut school altogether and get a dishwashing job. *Start on the bottom and work your way up,* that's what he'd say. Only most of the people he knew started on the bottom and worked their way sideways.

I got hooked watching cars swish by on the street. They'd skirt against the curb trying to crowd into a gas station at the corner. The pump man was this big, muscly guy with bleachy hair and angry clusters of pimples around his face and neck. He was tanking up the cars, banging the nozzle around like a cattleprod and pretty much doing a lousy job of wiping the windows. None of the customers seemed to work up a sweat about it, though, or maybe they just didn't want to

38

tussle with a beefy guy spitting sunflower seeds.

I was watching this when my old history teacher, Mr. Hart, came up and stood beside me. I remembered him because his favorite subject was the Civil War. He was wild about General McClellan, who he swore was a military genius and only needed a chance to put his sophisticated designs of warfare to work. Of course, on the battlefield, McClellan got chopped up bad by Robert E. Lee, but that didn't matter to Mr. Hart a bit; it was the beauty of the plan that counted. Once, I remember during class, after he'd gotten all teary-eyed about the battle of Gettysburg, this smart-aleck guy named Malcolm Augustus leaked out this cheesy little snicker and the whole class bursted out laughing. Mr. Hart's face pumped red with embarrassment.

At first he pretended he didn't recognize me, then he raised his eyebrows. "What are you doing here!?"

"I came to get my grades."

"What on earth for?"

He sounded concerned, so I told him. "My mom wants me to go Hawthorne School across town."

"Mmm," he said, looking down at my shoes.

"You *have* the grades. You're a pretty smart boy."
He was thinking hard, but he kept staring at my
shoes. They were my dad's old pair that had got
chewed up by dogs when he left them outside. My
feet slid around in two extra sizes of space. The
tongue flopped out of the left, and a jagged crack
split down the sole of the right from stomping on
shovels. Neither shoe had enough lace to grip
more than three rings.

"What have you been doing this summer?" Mr.
Hart asked finally, snapping out of his thoughts.

"I have been working in a variety of jobs."

I spoke organized English to Mr. Hart, maybe
a bit too organized. He was a twitchy kind of
teacher who got all pushed out of shape if you
talked to him natural. He was always wearing
stay-pressed slacks and a white shirt with a black
tie thin as an exclamation mark. I liked him
because he wasn't one of those movie-star
teachers who all the girls giggle over and guys
respect, who act like they're your buddy and want
to shoot the breeze when really they're just snoops
and end up reporting you for smoking in the
restroom.

"That's fine, real fine, Manuel," he said. "Most
kids don't carry their own weight, you know."

I shifted the shoe with the floppy tongue behind the other, regretting I'd worn them.

"How much money did you make for school?" he asked, smiling but holding back his teeth.

"Well, sir," I said, "we made enough."

Searching for words—mostly to keep his eyes away from my shoes—I told him we went to San Jose, but that was to pick figs, and only for a week. We never got to see the city.

Mr. Hart smiled again, still holding back his teeth, and rubbed his chin. He kept flicking at his nose, sliding out little flakes that he'd leave dangling. It looked awful.

"Did you ever stop to think, Manuel, that maybe you have to go places, experience things?"

"Well, sir, I never thought about it, actually."

He studied my shoes some more.

"How about it if I give you a ride home?" he said, rubbing the back of his hand.

Before I could unclog the surprise from my throat, he poked into his pocket and brought out a small paper bag and a pencil and scribbled something down.

"I'll be heading your way in a little while. Why don't you come with me."

Just then the bus came and I edged to the

curb, telling him thanks but no thanks. I talked with my hands to steer his eyes away from my shoes, but he kept staring. I was about to jump on the bus and bury myself in the crush of people when he smiled, this time agreeable and with a blare of teeth. He grabbed my arm, "Come on," he said. "You can keep me company."

My eyes followed the orange-lined bus as it pulled away from the curb. When I turned around, Mr. Hart was shaking his head and smiling at the ground where I'd been standing.

The school had been closed for summer, except for the administration building and some bungalows for half-day summer classes. Mr. Hart's room was on the second floor next to the typewriting class. Without all the ticking and tacking that goes on during regular school I could hear our footsteps whispering in the hallway.

Mr. Hart waved me into his office and asked where I lived. His room smelled salty; not ocean salty, or can of potted meat salty, but a musty, papery saltiness, like books sweating. He motioned me to sit down, but I stayed standing. Then he showed me what he had written on the paper bag. It said, *Give the Hernandez boy $20.* He pointed at the amount and asked if it was enough.

"Enough for what?"

"Enough for school supplies. You know, papers and pencils, binders, stuff like that. You'll need them at your new school." He was upping his voice to sound official.

Too embarrassed to tell him that attending another school was just a dream of my mom's— another one that probably wasn't going to hatch—I assured him that I had money by lightly patting my pocket. He nodded, then folded the paper. He reached back for his wallet anyway, and opened it to a spread of bills, tugging one out. Then, a shade embarrassed, and clearing his throat, he grabbed my hand and pretended to shake it, slipping me the money.

The sun was milky when we finally got going, and the air had a weight that made me swallow hard. Then a little wind came, but instead of being cool it snapped hot sparks in my face.

When we got to his car, Mr. Hart, antsy over the heat, revved the engine once and put it in gear. I cranked down the window as we pulled out of the parking lot, and the wind rolled in a small tidal wave of heat, splashing my face.

Mr. Hart decided against going down Chandler Avenue to the projects, where I lived. Instead, he took me in a roundabout journey across town, down Nestle Avenue, where he said I'd be going to school. From the window I could see the clean, green lawns of the houses closest to the road, the hoses neatly coiled, the driveways without a smear of oil. I'd only been there a few times to see the Christmas and Nativity scenes that during December were the main attractions. Antlered reindeers and cherry-cheeked Santas tramping on fake rooftop snow; Jesus as a swaddling baby; and camel caravans, complete with the Three Kings glowed among floodlights spread across the lawns. The whole avenue at that time of year was brilliant with lights and Christmas spangles.

I didn't really feel like talking. I mostly said "Yeah, yeah," whenever Mr. Hart shot his arms out to assemble some words above the steering wheel. There were houses behind forests of maple and pine trees that couldn't be seen from the road, except maybe a dip of a driveway or sun-splash of a window in the distance. I leaned my chin on the dashboard and asked, "Rich people live out here, huh?"

"It's just another place to live," Mr. Hart said blandly, "middle-class, some upper."

I could tell by the quickness of his voice that

he was disappointed that I was excited, except that I wasn't excited, but scared; scared of all the new kids I'd be meeting; different kids, the kind that lived in houses like these. Mr. Hart smiled and patted me on the shoulder.

"You're sure right about that, Mr. Hart," I said, nervously.

When we finally neared our projects, I asked him to drive around back and drop me off by the irrigation ditch near Frankie's house. He didn't know our project was lousy with snoops. People hanging outside on their front porches saw something suspicious in a white guy driving somebody home in a cream-colored car.

If my mom happened to be in the front yard, for instance, watering her plants, she'd have a heart attack for sure. She'd think somebody from the public housing works was coming to complain; or worse, think it was one of those unmarked police cars bringing her son home to psychologically torture her before locking me up forever.

Mr. Hart ignored me about dropping me off by Frankie's, and instead drove straight into the parking lot. Luckily, Mom wasn't home. But my dad was. When we pulled up he was plucking mint leaves by the water faucet. He zeroed his eyes angrily on me, and an icy, powerful mist began peeling away the inside walls of my lungs.

My dad had it in for white guys like Mr. Hart, who had good jobs and dressed in white shirts and black ties. It didn't matter that he was my teacher and that he was nice enough to give me a ride home. It didn't matter that, for whatever else one could say about him, Mr. Hart was an okay guy. What mattered to my dad was the possible panic I might cause my mom, or worse, that he'd be beholden to some white man for giving his son a ride home. No matter how many sophisticated ways I could turn it over to convince him, nothing would make sense to my dad. Letting Mr. Hart take me home was the worst acid I could have poured into his stomach.

He didn't say anything, though. When we got out of the car, he was sifting through the spearmint stems and shaking off the loose dirt with his thumbs. He did nod hello to Mr. Hart.

"How are you doing, sir," Mr. Hart said, walking across the yard. He stretched out his hand.

Oh no, I thought, *Dad's gonna flip him.* Instead he said, "Oh, fine, I'm doing real fine."

He said this good-naturedly, begging off Mr.

Hart's outstretched hand with a wave of the soily mint. With his mouth like clay that couldn't be massaged, he continued coolly prying apart the stems. When Mr. Hart turned to admire the yard, Dad lifted his eyes and gave me a look that could crack concrete.

You could tell Mr. Hart wanted to say something stupid, like how neat the yard was or what a fine impression our project house had on him. If he had, I think Dad would have mowed him down.

Luckily, he didn't say anything, and when he turned his back again, I put my head down quick. I could still feel Dad's eyes boring a hole through my skull. Toward Mr. Hart, though, he was a reservoir of calm water barely touched by the wind.

Finally, after a couple of minutes of nervously standing around, Mr. Hart waved a generous good-bye and tried again to shake Dad's hand. Dad just lifted the spearmint in one final excuse.

When Mr. Hart had gone, Dad came over and stared me square in the face. His eyes were dead and black, like a deep anger had eaten away the light. I wanted to run, but I couldn't signal my legs to move. My heart quickened as he threw down the spearmint and grabbed me roughly by the shoulders. He stuck his hand in my front shirt pocket. Being Nardo's hand-me-down shirt, it fit loose, and when Dad pulled, the pocket came down almost to my belly button. He yanked out a piece of smashed lint. Then he dug his fingers into my pants pockets and with grunting satisfaction pulled out the twenty-dollar bill.

"He give you this?" he asked, his voice croaking and the cords on his neck pulsing as he took in gulps of air. He didn't really expect an answer. He looked over at me with glazed eyes, then turned toward the house. As he reached the door, he swung back around and pointing right at the president's picture on the twenty-dollar bill, said, "Don't you think I know people like this?"

■4■

The Bullet

The twenty-dollar bill Dad took from me went into his drinking bankroll. Once he started a binge, he wouldn't stop until every cent drained from his pockets. For two days he didn't come home. On the second day, while we were sitting around the dinner table in front of some potatoes in red chili sauce and corn tortillas, our necks stiff, staring at the walls as if looking for scratches, Mom finally said we better go get him.

Having eaten only cornmeal that morning, my stomach gritting like hungry teeth, I sure wasn't in any mood to go to Rico's again. But I knew Mom. Until the problem of Dad was solved, she wouldn't let anybody eat. Already, the red chili sauce was thickening in the potatoes, and the corn tortillas were warping like records in the sun.

"Could you take care of the baby while we're gone?" Mom asked Magda, whose eyes stabbed angrily back at her. They'd been arguing all morning, and had established a polite buffer of silence between them.

At the pool hall, when Mom and I walked in through the doors, Dad's friends lifted their heads and rolled their eyes, pushing back their hair. Rico, who was always fidgeting with his collar, dropped his hands and cleared his throat. He had his hair combed in a pompadour and had the look of a finicky barber. Mom asked about Dad, and Rico, tapping his finger on the counter, said he'd gone home.

It was the way he said it, too nonchalant, too nervously offhand, too guilty, actually, that made Mom suspicious right away. She began roving her eyes around the bar in a slow wandering arc, then walked straight as a divining rod into the men's restroom. There she found Dad hiding in a toilet stall.

Although she really didn't want to embarrass him in front of his cronies, and even though Dad came out looking cool and unfluttered, you could tell he'd been cut down a notch. He went to the counter proud as possible and ordered a beer. Rico said he couldn't spare any more credit.

Hearing this, and turning around on his bar stool, Mr. Sanchez, our neighbor from the projects, said, "Mano, I'll buy you beer." He was sitting at the bar, and when he pulled out his money he almost flopped off his bar stool.

Rico twirled a quarter that spilled out of Sanchez's pocket. "Keep your money," he said, "Manuel has to go home."

"No, no, I want to buy him a drink," Mr. Sanchez said sincerely, as only someone who'd been drinking can.

"No, he is going home with his wife," Rico said, mildly insistent. In the light of the pool hall, the waves of his brilliantined hair shone like glints of tar. He strained a smile of apology at Mom, who touched her hair like it was a mess. Then Dad slapped his hand hard on the counter, startling them both, and shouted, "If I want a beer, I can have a beer!"

Rico just stared at him, unblinking.

Dad was sore, but not stoked enough to start shoving anybody around. At worst maybe he'd throw a few fake tomahawk chops at me. He turned to me like he was going to do just that, but stopped himself. "Ahhh, *el perico*. How are you doing today, *Perico*?"

Perico, or parrot, was what Dad called me sometimes. It was from a Mexican saying about a parrot that complains how hot it is in the shade, while all along he's sitting inside an oven. People usually say this when talking about ignorant people who don't know where they're at in the world. I didn't mind it so much, actually, because Dad didn't say it because he thought I was dumb, but because I trusted everything too much, because I'd go right into the oven trusting people all the way—brains or no brains.

That's when Mom began to sense that Dad was angrier than he was letting on. She grabbed me by the shoulder and steered me out the door. Some girls were coming out of the Azteca Theater down the street, giggling, pulling on each other's braids, and there was a station wagon parked on the curb loaded with about ten noisy kids. When I looked back I saw Dad through the window lean forward on the counter, rubbing his chin like it was sore.

Mom hurried me along, whisking her head back every once in a while to see if Dad was following. Her lips were twisting funny and churning on words I couldn't hear above the hum of car tires. Stretching my T-shirt, she hurried me along with shoves, a couple of times even punching me on the shoulder. Each car grinding its gears on the street I thought was Dad pulling up beside us and ordering us inside the car. Tiny splinters of light were flittering away from the grass when we got back to the projects.

Right away Mom told Magda, who was putting cold cream on her face, to go visit Linda, her girlfriend who lived down the block. She didn't have to tell her twice. It took about three seconds for Magda to rush out the door, wiping cold cream off her face with a towel.

Mom figured Dad would come home in a lousy mood, but that he wouldn't do anything to me, since really, deep down Dad liked me. She told me to stay home and watch over Pedi, who was asleep, then wrote something on a piece of paper, folded it, and laid it on the table.

When he came home, Dad threw his cigarette on the porch and stubbed it with his heel. The evening air must have built back the balance in his legs, because he was walking straighter. He was swishing and slapping a chinaberry branch against his pant leg. He pulled out another cigarette, but left it dead and bobbing on his lips.

Because Mom sometimes polished the floor in the late afternoon, he was careful to not step into any scary, heart-fluttering slides. Once inside the door, he strained to see in the half light, then leveled the stick under his eye, signaling that I should go to my room.

When he was working for the city, every payday Dad used to come home lugging in boxes of groceries. He'd walk into the living room, and all the pictures, tiny statues and glass animals Mom collected would sparkle from the light rushing in through the door. It was like his coming home made them sparkle. Now he came home late, usually, with nothing—no rent money, no car money, no food money, no sparkle. And mostly he came home drunk, his face drowsy with booze, rambling about how he lost his job, or how the pain in his back felt like a broken-tooth gear, cranking and cranking.

Dad tossed the stick onto the couch. He began talking to himself in this polite, official voice. He sometimes unlocked this voice from under his tongue when he wanted to pump his words up to impress himself. It also meant he wanted to distance himself from us, to make us all strangers, so that nothing we said could touch him.

"I'm home!" he announced, loudly. "I said, 'I'm home.' Did you hear me?" He looked at the floor, and although it was scrubbed clean, acted like there was a surf of dirt rising to his ankles. "What is this? What is this mess? How can a man come home to a mess like this?"

He roamed his eyes around the kitchen, opening his arms as if expecting the walls to agree with him. He took a step toward me, then changed his mind and sat down at the yellow Formica table. The paper on the table was still creased but folded open, because I'd read it.

"What the hell is this, goddamn it?" he said. He flicked down his unlit cigarette and picked up the paper. "She wants to leave me. That's what she wants to do," he said, glancing at the paper and tossing it back on the table.

"No, she doesn't, Dad," I said. "She says she went to get her hair done at Sophie's."

Burying his hands in his pockets and cradling in his shoulders, like he was cold, Dad said, "That *pinche* Sophie, filling her head with ideas." His face, which he'd kept alert since walking through the door, softened, and his eyes floated around the kitchen. Then he got up and veered down the hallway, a skirt of hair oil, beer and cigarette smoke wafting in the ammonia air. He paused at the door of his room. "I'll fix her," he said.

Dad pulled out his rifle from the shelf of his closet, and after checking the loader began searching for bullets, waking up Pedi, who groaned and rubbed her eyes. He swung open the bathroom cabinet, his drunk hand shoveling and knocking over toothbrushes, shaving cream, half-empty bottles of cologne that he'd always buy and never finish. Remembering all the places where Mom hid his liquor bottles, he stumbled around opening cupboards, reaching far back into shelves and behind pipes under the kitchen sink. He scattered Mom's animal collection, slapping her little glass and ceramic cows, pigs, donkeys, even rhinos and an elephant off the shelves. With one swoosh of his arm, he thrashed to the floor my green plastic tyrannosaurus.

I was behind him all the way, picking up and putting things back the best I could, trying not to trample over Pedi, awake and helping Dad look for the bullets. I was begging him to please respect reason, but quickly found myself saying, "But Dad, if you shoot Mom, they'll only throw you in jail. Then what will happen to us?"

"I don't care what happens to you," Dad clipped, "only Pedi. Isn't that right, *mija*?" he said to Pedi. "You're the only one your dad cares about?"

Pedi was really awake now, and excited, working her legs and stabbing her chubby hands in the air. In the pantry, she tipped over cans of tomatoes and string beans. She thought Daddy was playing a game, that he was going to show her how to shoot the gun. She wanted to hear it go *khurrr*, like in the movies. She wanted to see something collapse at the end of the barrel when the sound trailed off.

"Pedi, cut that out!" I said.

"You shut up! My *mija* is helping me, not you!" Dad said, kicking away clothes that he'd flung out of the closet.

"Dad," I said, trying to be calm. "You have to understand, you'll only get in trouble.... ."

My words weren't worth a penny in his ears.

"I don't care about trouble," he said. "It's that *bruja*, that witch, I've had it up to here with her." He jerked the rifle up to show how high he'd had it up to with my mom and smacked the barrel against his forehead. He shifted the rifle to his other hand and touched the hurt, relieved when his fingers came away clean.

He found some bullets, finally, inside Mom's dresser drawer, knotted up in one of her old bras. In his anxiousness to untie the straps, he scattered the bullets all over the floor. Rocking a little on his heels, he waited for Pedi to pick them up. She could get into corners and at one that spun like a pinwheel under the bed. I also picked up a bullet, but stashed it in my pocket.

"Here you go, Daddy, here," Pedi gushed, handing him three copper-headed .22 bullets. She ducked her head down and was about to scurry for more when Dad stepped out the door. "Wait, Daddy, wait for me!" Pedi yelled, running down the hall after him. At the door, Dad strained the hydraulic screen wide, and when it sprung back, it slammed against Pedi's face. She fell back on her butt and began to cry.

"Oh, Pedi, you stupid!" I said, then rushed out searching for Dad.

The sky was a soft glow, pushing the houses, trees and electric posts forward in relief. I found Dad hammering on the kitchen door of Sophie's house, swearing at Sophie and Mom to quit being cowards and let him in. The lights of the kitchen blinked off, blacking the house, but then turned on again and another weaker light came on in the living room.

I rushed over to the front just in time to see Mom bolt across the porch, scared out of her mind. She had pink roller sponges cinched into her hair and an apron tied clumsily around her neck. Bobby pins dangled from her half-finished curls. She knew Dad was angry. She was just trying to blossom herself up, but Dad didn't understand that. He didn't know how awful she felt about embarrassing him at the pool hall. She ran toward the crowd of maple trees where the trunks were thick and black against the soft night.

I yelled, "Mom!" and realized my mistake right away. Dad heard me, and came swerving around the corner. He was trying to slide a bullet into the chamber of the rifle, but it slipped through his fingers onto the ground. He left it there in a dark cradle of dirt and tried another, but that one got stuck in the loader. He wrestled with the bolt arm. "Where? Where's your mother?" he said, stumbling.

"Over there!" I yelled, pointing to the other side of Sophie's house.

Dad didn't even turn to where I pointed. From the corner of his eye, he caught the dark clump of Mom running, and ran after her. When she disappeared behind a tree, he froze, shifting his knees, the barrel of the rifle alert and ready. For an instant I caught a glimpse of her tiptoeing away from a tree. Dad saw her too and banged on the bolt arm. She started with a jolt and began running again, ducking and dodging from tree to tree, as Dad, frustrated with the loader because it wouldn't eat the bullet, and not wanting her to escape, pretended to lock a bullet in the chamber and level aim. He even lifted the barrel and made a shooting noise with his lips. *Kapow. Kapow.* Mom flinched her shoulders every time he did it, too.

Then I heard the police. Not the siren of the police or the *blink blink* of quick lights, but the hush of deep-threaded tires pressing against asphalt, an engine that wound and gathered like a powerful animal. I felt a pressure in my throat, and my legs were full of cement. "Get back to the house," I yelled in a thick voice. "Get back to the house!"

Dad stopped and turned around. He saw the police car pulling up from the street bordering our projects, then the lights, *flash flash,* and rushed back toward the house.

"Come on, Mom," I shouted, waving her in like into home plate. "The police are coming!" She started bustling toward me. When she passed me, she was breathing fast and her hair smelled of perm solution.

When we got back to the house, Dad was standing in the middle of the living room like he was lost, the rifle dangling in his right hand. Mom snatched up Pedi, still whimpering, and smacked her on the butt to get her moving. She splashed the curtains shut, and turned off the lamp, then headed for the hallway. Before reaching it, we all heard police shoes grating on the sidewalk, and Mom turned quickly toward Dad, who was holding the rifle like it was too much weight for him. I thought she was going to slap him, but instead she wrestled the rifle out of his hands and ran with it down the hallway.

That's when the two cops arrived. Seeing Dad through the screen door, they stiffened, pressing their hands against their leather holsters. But then they loosened their shoulders when they saw that he was just standing there. They slowly stretched back the hydraulic door and came into the room, crouching at the knees, just to be safe, their eyes roving around.

Unfortunately, they also saw Mom's shadow against the hallway wall, shoved out by the light of Magda's room. She must have been frozen there, wondering what to do with the rifle. I thought the police were going to panic and start shooting, thinking maybe Mom was there to ambush them, but they seemed to guess right away what was going on.

When Mom moved away, the cop in front asked Dad about the rifle. He was a large man with burly arms, soft with a yellow fur of hair. The two stomach buttons on his shirt were open wide enough to stick a softball through.

"What rifle?" Dad said, trying to straighten himself to appear sober.

"Are you Mr. Hernandez?"

"Yes, officer, I am," Dad said, tossing his hand in the air.

"Well, sir," said the policeman. "We have a report here that a man from this house was pointing a weapon around the neighborhood." He switched on a flashlight, and flicked the beam around the room, lighting a moon on Mom's glass-top table and pausing on the large picture of the Last Supper, framed in gold plastic and with cherub angels mounted on each corner. Then he relaxed his wrist and crossed the beam from Dad to me with a careless flicker.

"I don't know what you're talking about," Dad said.

"The report we received, Mr. Hernandez, claims you were trying to shoot your wife."

"That's crazy! My wife's over there." He pointed to Mom, who came down the hallway with Pedi, her eyes big as wheels, clutching at her skirt.

"Mrs. Hernandez?" the officer asked, as if trying to make her out in the dark.

Mom nodded, shielding her hair. She pressed at a drooping curl near her ear and glanced over at Dad, who dropped his eyes.

"Mrs. Hernandez," the officer said again, lifting his fist to his mouth and letting out a loud, ratchety cough, "as I was explaining to your husband, we received a report that a man was trying to shoot his wife. The report mentions this address and both your names."

Mom didn't say anything. Instead, she raised her eyes to the ceiling, breathing deep, as if gathering enough air to blow up a balloon. She stood like that for a while, hands on her hips, holding in her lungs. Her face appeared calm and lifted, as if she were listening to soft guitar music from far away.

Both officers studied her curiously and exchanged glances, the one in back still alert, his hand stiff on his holster and thumb cocked like a talon over the gun hammer.

Mom's curious silence nudged Dad into a small panic. "We don't know what you're talking about, officer," he said, shuffling toward her. "No one is trying to do anything here. Besides, we don't have a gun. Rebecca, tell him we don't have a gun."

Her eyes, which had opened wide from holding in her breath, blinked and glazed over, then she released the air from her lungs and began breathing deeply, evenly, fingering a curl of hair near her ear. Dad egged her again with his palm to please say something, but she only stared at a blank spot on the wall.

"You can see nothing's wrong here, officer," Dad said, nervously.

"Well, Mr. Hernandez, the truth is, that when we came in through the door, we saw your wife here taking away what looked to us like a firearm."

"But we don't have a firearm," Dad said again, trying to staunch their worries.

The first officer grimaced suspiciously, then he raised his flashlight and nodded to the other who, with eyes shifting and hand still braced on his pistol, walked past Mom and disappeared down the hallway. We all stood there—Dad, Mom, Pedi, the first officer, and me—looking, not looking at each other. A moment later, the other officer came out holding the .22.

"I found it in the last room, under the bed," he said, waving it in the air in reluctant triumph.

The first officer slowly shook his head and sighed, rubbing his finger reflectively along a deep crease on his forehead. "Now, Mr. Hernandez. I don't want to hear any more about how we don't have a rifle, because there's obviously a rifle here. And I don't want to hear anything about this particular rifle *not* being yours, because I'm fairly sure that it is." He sighed again and with a slow shake of his head took the rifle from the other officer's hand. He shined the flashlight on it, inspecting it, turning it over in his hand and squinching his eyes at a mark under the barrel.

"Mr. Hernandez," he said, finally, straightening his shoulders. "I don't want to have to tell you this, but I'm sorry, we're going to have to confiscate this rifle."

I saw ice freeze around Dad's eyes. "You can't take my rifle," he said abruptly, in a voice I knew meant trouble.

"Mr. Hernandez," the officer said, unbinding his shoulders some more, "there doesn't seem to be any registration number on this rifle. It's against the law to have an unregistered firearm."

That's when Mom, dragging Pedi along with her, went over and stuck her finger inside Dad's belt loop.

Seeing this, the first officer waved a cautious hand at her and stepped over to his partner. He leaned into his ear, nodded and turned back to Dad. "Mr. Hernandez, we're taking the rifle. If you want it back, you'll have to come to the station. But I don't advise you do that, sir. I really don't. I'm sure the Chief will want to ask a lot more questions about this rifle."

"Don't take it," Dad said. His voice was thick, and he was beginning to breathe harder. I saw a redness flow up the vein of his neck and gather in a puddle of wine under his ear.

That's when Mom pulled on his belt loop, enough to bend him a bit at the waist, and to my relief Dad loosened a little. "Look," he said, more calmly, "you can't take it. I wasn't doing anything."

The officer narrowed his eyes and lowered the rifle along his leg. He tucked his chin into his shoulder and signaled with one eye to the other officer, who instantly became alert. "I'm sorry then, Mr. Hernandez," he said, "we're going to have to take you in for possession of an illegal firearm."

Before any more talk, and moving as if studying his own movements, the second officer walked over to Mom and slowly, as if trying to be polite, lifted her hand away from Dad's belt loop. Then with a smooth, relaxed quickness, he took hold of Dad's arms and just like that handcuffed him. Dad seemed to be stunned into feebleness by the speed in which the officer worked. All he could say was "You can't take my rifle . . . you can't take my rifle," his voice sinking into a plea.

The first officer turned to Mom and raised a hand of apology. "Mrs. Hernandez, I sure am sorry about this. I sure am, believe me."

But Mom wasn't listening. She seemed to still be hearing something in the air. Then her face became more alert, and she turned to the officer leading Dad out of the door. "Take him," she said, softly at first, then with decided anger. "Go ahead, take him!"

After the police had gone, Mom sat on the couch a long time staring at the floor. I noticed that she didn't appear tired, but more like the muscles needed to move her face were numb. The curtains were closed, and there were no lights, but my eyes adjusted to the dark. The walls of the room, like in all the houses in our neighborhood, were Sheetrock, painted white, but in the darkness everything looked gray. The frame of the Last Supper, with its gold-colored flange and cherub angels, looked as gray as a plastic-model battleship. Even the glass-top table mirrored a reflection of gray.

Seeing a dark spot on the floor, Mom bent over and picked up a little donkey, staring at it, and delicately turning it over in her fingers as if expecting a hoof to suddenly click off. "You know," she said, "I don't even have a vacuum cleaner. Sophie has a vacuum cleaner. So does Mrs. Lopez. When the police came, I heard Mrs. Lopez's vacuum cleaner. It sounded like it was really picking up dirt."

Ever since seeing a demonstration by a plaid-suited man who came to our door, Mom had always wanted a vacuum cleaner. The man threw dirt and cigarette ash on our bathroom drop rug and to our amazed eyes sucked it all away. "There's an attachment you can hold in your hand," he had said. "That way you can get into cabinets and corners. You don't need any cloth rags. You don't need a broom. It does all the work for you."

My legs weakened, like someone had pulled a plug from my ankles and drained all my energy, so I sat down on the couch. "Mom," I said, "Mom. . . ."

She wasn't listening. She lay back on the couch and lifted her arm, resting it on her forehead, as if the heat were unbearable.

"Mom," I said again. "When do you think they're going to let Dad out?"

"When I go pay the bail."

"How much is the bail?"

"I don't know. But it's too much, I know that." Her voice sounded muffled, as though she were talking through stuffed cotton. She carefully placed the donkey on the glass table. "They'll just have to let him out when they decide to let him out."

After sitting quietly there with Mom for a while, I got up and went into Pedi's room. Her face was moist and fevery, and she was whimpering. All the excitement had opened up something bad inside her, and with her two fists

69

pressed tightly against her chest, she was trying to close it. I reached into my pocket and pulled out the bullet I'd picked up earlier and wedged it between her fingers. That seemed to quiet her a little.

The Garden

eep down I hoped Mom would wise up and leave Dad for good, or maybe go live with Grandma for a while, or run off on her own, if that's what she wanted. Either that, or that Dad would finally open his eyes to see how close it was to being his last chance. But none of what I wished was going to happen.

On the day Dad got out of jail, Mom ordered us to clean this and clean that, she was so excited. Singing church hymns she learned as a girl, she took a long bath with some of Magda's creamy soap, and dusted powder on her neck and shoulders. We went on the bus to pick him up, and after we returned home, I lingered in the living room reading my science magazine. I'd found it thrown away in the alley behind Giddens's Pharmacy, a big boot print tracking the front cover, and its slippery paper warped by rain, but still amazing with pictures of flashy-colored planets whirling around in a thick, black space, and grinning dinosaurs fighting.

All afternoon they talked over the kitchen

table about how things were going to get better. Dad promised he'd never go anywhere unless he said what time he'd be back, and how he was going to find a job and not just look for a job, since looking for a job kept him at the pool hall with all the other guys just looking for jobs. Mom promised she would never again embarrass him in front of his friends. And some other things I couldn't make out. Finally, when they were done promising each other everything, night was beginning to push away the light, and they went to sleep, laying slowly down on their squeaky bed.

After staying up for the longest time, with everything inside me scary and about to collapse, I heard rustling outside by the elm tree, and then Nardo's round face appeared at the window. He was drunk, mushy around the mouth, his eyes watery and stained. After losing his grip and stumbling a couple of times, he finally hoisted his belly over the window ledge and flopped into the room. He rose clumsily to his feet, and sat on the bed, staring at the floor as if over a cliff. He tried to take off his shoes but only knotted the laces. Seeing me awake, he started to ask about Dad, but I shushed him with my finger.

"Well," he said, swaying, "did he get out?"

"He got out, now shut up!" I hissed.

He sat there staring at me for a while. "What??? Are they going to make it all right again?"

"That's what they say."

"Yeah, those two, they're crazy, you know that? They're crazy."

"They ain't as crazy as you," I said, rolling over and covering my shoulder, then turning back around. "If you keep talking, they're going to come in here and gang up on you."

"Like I care."

"You better care, because I think they'd rather be fighting with you than with each other. If I was you, I'd lay down and go to sleep."

Nardo curled his arm around the bedpost and smiled. "Yeah, that's funny. That sure is funny," he said, moving his head up and down. "They'll probably be picking fights with us tomorrow, huh?"

"Shut up and go to sleep," I said, tiredly.

He looked at the mirror over by the door and noticed a swirl of his hair out of place. He tried clumsily to press it down but it kept popping up. Then he walked over to the mirror and peered

73

into it, as if noticing something he hadn't before, pointing a lazy finger at himself. For a long time he stared at the mirror, pointing, then walked slowly back to his bed and plopped down, asleep.

I woke to the bare bulb stinging my eyes. It was morning, and Dad was in the room, breathing heavy, like he'd just gotten out of a shower. He grunted at me and roughly shook Nardo awake, who got up digging his fists in his eyes, still starched from drinking the night before. Dad slid out his belt from around the loops of his pants and began slapping it against the mattress, threatening to burn our legs if we didn't listen. He stood around bullying us into our clothes and without breakfast drove us to Grandma's.

Dad must have sizzled on some smart plans while he was in jail, and now, after all the smooth talk with Mom was over, he was ready to get into action. I'd rather have gotten dragged across a cactus desert and dropped thirsty in a lake of salt than listen to him, but he had us there in the car, muscling his voice so our minds wouldn't wander.

Grandma lived in a clapboard house at the corner of two old gray roads that the city, after scrimping for years, finally paved over with asphalt. The asphalt came cheap, without curbs, and on the first dangerous sun it melted and became lumpy. From then on cars driving over it jostled in a chorus of springs, and people's heads bounced wildly.

Dad pushed the car door open, leaned back on the seat and said he wanted the yard raked and hoed before he came back. "And I mean spotless," he said, pointing a menacing finger at us. He leaned over and slammed the door shut.

Cleaning a yard to my dad meant even the grass edges had to be trimmed and plants polished. He reminded us that he'd check on our work, making sure we dug out to his satisfaction the tufts of grass near Grandma's roses and pinched out whatever mealy bugs and aphids were chewing on the stems. We could tell it was going to be one of those hot days when asphalt softens and ants foam up from the dirt with the scratch of a stick, and when dogs bark, the sound is dry, like hollow wood. But it was still morning, and the first hour was a smile and thoughts of lunch; nothing but a few shrubs to chop and leaves to rake.

Nardo had trouble coming back from his hangover. He moved like a ground sloth, and kept gulping water from the garden hose. He sobered up a little when we began to clip off the small yellow weeds choking the roses. The bigger shoots over by the *nopal* cactus had to be pulled. The roots sunk deep and we knew in a month they'd spring up again, so we pulled with every muscle until a big chunk of the main stalk plucked out.

We wore our arms out pulling those weeds, as well as stacking the bricks Dad had once stored in the corner of the yard to build a barbecue pit. We found a couple of centipedes numb underneath an old plank and crushed them under our heels. We sent chips soaring from the axe as we cut out the roots of a dead trunk and dropped its bulk thundering into a wheelbarrow.

When Horacio, my grandma's cat, came around, we were chopping the last weeds growing inside the flowerbeds. Nardo called to him, but he was stalking near the cherry tree. When the chirp of a bird skeetered in the air, he stiffened, his nose twitching and ears cupped like radar antennae, then he darted away, clawing up the tree trunk.

When we stopped, finally, the sun was prickling like a hot rash on the back of my neck, and a piece of lava was wedged in my spine. My brother's face was swollen and burnished as a new penny. A channel of sweat slipped down the bridge of his nose and plopped on the dirt near his feet. His eyes, drowsy with sun, watched it like someone who didn't deserve sweat.

"Hey, you know what?" he said, stretching. He pulled his shoulders back and the muscles tightened under his T-shirt. With one last punch of the hoe, he exploded a puff of dirt. "I'm gonna get some Kool-Aid. How about that? You want some Kool-Aid?"

"Why don't we finish first, we only got this to do," I said, knowing that once he went inside, work was over. I looked at the cherry tree standing brilliant at the end of the garden, its leaves twirling and echoing light. It wasn't just a cherry tree. Long ago Grandpa had chopped off limbs and grafted saplings of different fruit. One branch sprouted plums, another almonds, and still another, peaches. Most were cherries, though. When in season, they glowed ripe and flashed like Christmas balls.

"I'll wait for you right over there," I said, pointing to the tree.

"No, you just keep on working, I'll be right back. Don't worry, I'll be right back." Nardo made a move to leave, but seeing me straighten up, he put his hand assuringly on my shoulder. "Don't you believe me?" he asked. "I *said* I'll be right back."

"No, I *believe* you," I said. "I just want to make sure you're not going to take a nap."

"I'm not gonna take a nap! What's the matter with you, anyway?" he asked. "You been so suspicious lately. You act like I'm gonna quit or something."

When I didn't say anything, he slid the hoe along his knee, levered it in the air, then snatched it quickly by the neck. "I'll be right back, believe me!"

It was no use arguing with Nardo. He could go around the same point from twenty different angles. "You do what you want," I said, waving my hand like it weighed a ton, "but I'm going to sit down."

Now that I'd given up, he was pretty springy. He hurdled the back steps in one leap and stopped at the door. "Man," he said, smiling, "and they call *me* lazy."

I shuffled over to the faucet, swishing the dirt from my pants. My joints felt slack, and my lips were cracked enough to bleed if I mouthed a zero.

I'd taken my shirt off hours ago, and when I pressed my finger against the skin of my shoulder, I felt the numb warning of sunburn. Splashing water on myself came to mind, but my neck and shoulders chilled at the thought. Instead I hosed water into the cup of my hands and washed my face, drying it with my shirt before putting it back on.

As the sun winked over the ledge of the roof, the shadows of the cherry tree stretched across the yard, smudging Grandma's row of cactus. Pinching the waterspout, I flecked some water on them and watched as curling wisps of hot dust exploded from the spiked, green skin.

When Nardo came back, he had two clinking glasses in one hand and an ice pitcher of Kool-Aid in another. He watched the clouds herding west and frowned at the puddle of water foaming like dirty milk near the faucet.

"Are you gonna work anymore or what?" he asked, accusingly.

"No," I said, inspecting my fingernails, half-mooned with dirt.

"Hell then, let's quit." He hunched back his shoulders and blew up his lungs; then, tilting his head back, he began drinking from the pitcher in huge, noisy gulps. Then he filled a glass and finished that, shaking the purple-stained ice cubes. He put the pitcher on a wood stool nearby.

"Besides," he said, breathing heavy, "Grandma's awake."

"Grandma's awake?"

"Yeah." He pressed his arms against his sides, feigning fear. "She said she just woke up from a dream where Grandpa was sitting on the bed beside her."

He lay down on the shaded grass, linking his fingers behind his neck. Like my dad's, his hair was swirly and glinted in the sun like splashes of water. I looked at the muscles along his ribs where the T-shirt had ridden up and thought of my own flabby waist. Nardo only had a mulberry birthmark on his shoulder, which he always rubbed when thinking. I had a face Dad said would look handsome on a horse.

Grandma came around from the front wearing a flowery Japanese kimono. Her eyes weren't too strong, so she groped around, homing in on our faces. Ropes pulled at her from the ground when she walked and her sighs sounded like roots releasing from moist earth.

Nardo put the pitcher on the ground and

brought Grandma the stool, which she stared at a while before sitting down. It belonged to my grandpa, who had died some years back after his brain got fevery and he couldn't recognize anyone, even himself in the mirror when we held it up one day for him to comb his hair. A sickness broke down the muscles in his legs, then broke down the stories about Mexico that smoldered in his heart. In the end, his only memory was of the desert he crossed to plant his foot in this country.

Grandma used to keep her face pretty like a baby doll, dabbing cold cream on it every night. She used to tighten her hair in knots and dye it black like a young girl's. Now her face was webbed with wrinkles, and her hair sworly white and frazzled. She still sprinkled on perfume, and was still wild about painting her lips, except now the sprinkles became palmfuls and the lipstick wandered, smearing her face eerie.

She gazed dreamily over the yard. It was beautiful back then, she said. It was a garden, and every house had one so bright a person's eyesight blurred. She remembered browsing among the flowers, smelling odors that even people in heaven would envy. My brother and I scanned around, trying to imagine the same wonder, but what we saw wasn't as sweet as Grandma remembered. I even tried to imagine neighbors, which she no longer had, except far down the road. One by one, they had all moved away.

She must have sensed our confusion, because she said it was true, the yard wasn't as joyful as when she and Grandpa were young. She said it was mostly the drought that sucked all the gardens away, but we knew that wasn't altogether true. There were still reservoirs of water, even if the rings showed how much the drought had shrunk them. It was more that the city planned to build a freeway, and was slowly buying and wrecking the houses, plowing the gardens gray. Grandpa and his neighbor, Mr. Vuksanivich, refused to sell, and for a while the city held back its plans for a freeway. Grandpa kept the garden alive and Mr. Vuksanivich kept his pasture green. Then Mr. Vuksanivich died, and the city bought the land from his son, and then Grandpa also died, and with him, the garden. Since Mom was the oldest, my dad figured she'd get the house when Grandma died.

The sun was a spot of dried blood on the rim of the horizon when Grandma waved at the cherry tree with her finger. *"Allí,"* she said. "There." A few puckered cherries lay on the ground; a mantis unfurled a blue sail and skittered across the grass. "There," she said, again. "There!"

Long ago, under the drooping branches, was once a small girl, our mother, with a handkerchief covering her dark, pony eyes. She was swinging a stick at a bull *piñata* slung on a rope. By a chance hit, she burst open the clay pot nestled inside the bull's belly. Fistfuls of chocolates and candy came cascading out of the wound. Everyone screamed with excitement. The children, from the once full neighborhood of children, scurried about, eyes watery and chubby hands stashing candies into their pockets. They laughed with a cute, greedy look Grandma said only a child can make. *"Qué curiositos se miraban,"* she said. "How curious they looked."

Grandma Rosa died a few months later, and after the burial we gathered at her house. The sun was as bright as an egg yolk leaking an orange finger across a porcelain plate, and there was a smell of bruised plums and burning grapevines drifting through the trees.

My aunt Letty cried so loud my uncle Joe scolded her by twirling his finger. "Now, now

Leticia," he said to her, "there's nothing you can do for her now." With a shredded throat, Letty told him to shut up.

Although moist around the cheeks, Mom didn't cry. She sat on the living room couch next to the shuffling cooler. She didn't wear black because she had no black dress, and my dad could only scrounge up seven dollars and twenty-eight cents. Mom claimed this was as good as could be expected, considering the funeral costs, but not half enough for a respectable black dress. She used the money instead to buy Mexican sweet bread, and make *buñuelos,* fried tortillas sprinkled with cinnamon, and sweet potatoes that bled a dark syrup.

Sitting there, Nardo, my cousin Rio and I stared at Grandma's old chair. I remembered once sleeping on the floor and a mouse scuttling across my stomach. I awoke to see Grandma under the tulip lamp, asleep, her head circled by a glowing moon of light. Then I heard scuffling, as a mouse scratched across on the wooden floor. Suddenly, there was a cushiony thud, and the mouse let out a tiny, piercing *yeek,* as though driven through with an icepick. It was Horacio, my grandma's cat, who'd spotted the mouse from his perch on the mantel and pounced on it, pinning it between his claws. As my eyes brightened in the dark, I saw Horacio's fur glowing, as he sort of smiled down at the mouse. Then he released it, and it scurried away to search for a hole; but Horacio leaped again, clasping and pawing the mouse around the floor like a ball of yarn. I watched in fascination as he let the mouse go three or four times, rolling it around with crisp, playful precision until he finally snatched it up and throddled it down his throat, the tail churning around his mouth.

Grandma's chair had bark designs on its wooden legs and carved bear claws for handrests. Already frayed on the cushion, wobbly in the struts, its wooden legs scratched, no one except Grandma ever sat in it. I began wondering about what would happen to it now that it was empty of her.

I leaned forward on the couch and in a half whisper told Nardo that the night before I had dreamt about Grandma. She and I were walking together in the mountains, when suddenly, under our feet, a huge earthquake erupted, with fire tearing open the earth like a sharp knife through seams of old leather. I woke up shivering and soaked in cold sweat. The walls of my room were like blue ice, like the sky after a clean rain.

Dreams fascinated Nardo. He could analyze people's sleep. Grandma claimed this was because he had a birthmark in the shape of an eagle's wing on his shoulder. Nardo said that before leaving for heaven the dead sometimes sprinkle messages inside the ears of those they love. He didn't know why Grandma would want to leave a message for me, but the dream sounded like a warning. I would die alone, he predicted, in a very cold place.

I leaped from the couch and hammered him on the arm. We wrestled around the living-room floor in front of Mom, too buried in her grief to pay us any mind. Dad wasn't too buried in grief, though. Irked by our noisy tumbling, he burst in from the kitchen and with one of his shoes, crowned us both on the head. He pointed the shoe threateningly at everybody and said that we all better get the message quick about how to behave, or else.

After Dad's scolding, we sat quietly on the couch across from Mom. She was looking down at the floor as if searching for scuff marks. We all became bored and antsy. My cousin Rio pretended to be mournful, and Nardo coolly studied the dust on the windowpane, grinning because the blow Dad had given him hadn't even hurt.

Only Pedi was having fun. She came into the room revving her lips like an airplane and spanning her arms. She circled us at an angle, swooping past Nardo and snagging her wing on his pants pocket. She flew on a crippled half wing a little way before crashing.

When she started playing at making faces, we giggled, but stopped when Dad poked his head in from the kitchen. "I'm gonna *burn* somebody's legs," he warned.

Everybody really shut up after that and stared at the walls. I munched on a sweet potato and gazed at the ringed stains inside my coffee cup. Finally, ignoring everybody's eyes licking after my heels, I snuck out the door.

Outside, the air was a sleek powdery ash. It dusted Dad's car and uncle Joe's panel truck, parked grille to grille on the gravel driveway. Steam rose from the hoods in thin ghostly clouds, and blanched by the sun, the windshields shone like morning frost. I climbed over the hood of my uncle's truck and walked over to the cherry tree, clambering up on a branch.

Over the wood shingles of the house, I could

see a blond strip of Mr. Vuksanivich's old pasture. The grapevines had been plowed over and the house lifted on struts, then trucked away, but I could almost see old Mr. Vuksanivich standing there in a gray sweater, raking and burning leaves, a great plume of smoke rising into a cloud.

In the kitchen, I heard Dad talking loud. Everybody else's voices made tiny booms of sound against the walls, but my dad's voice cut through the walls. He was talking to my uncle Joe about how impossible it was going to be to keep up the place, and how he'd have to sell it. You could almost hear the strategies sizzling around inside his head, like hot sand swirling inside a tin cup.

I sat there imagining the cherry tree's roots slithering down into the earth, and how it would have to be pulled out by a strong tractor; and also, I thought about how, in the end, Grandma couldn't read anymore under the tulip lamp, only sit on her armchair, looking up at the ceiling, swallowing and swallowing; and once, when she put her arm on my shoulder, I felt the dead weight of her strength abandoning her.

In my family, we're taught to touch the hand of the one who has died. So at the wake, when my mother called, I walked toward the casket, and in the full bloom of my family's eyes, I touched Grandma's hand. A lump of salt caught in my throat, closing like a fist, as I studied the bark skin of her face—each crack sealed with perfect makeup.

She will flake away into dirt, I thought, just as the sun does the bottom of a pond during a drought. Her shadow will be erased, and her soul will drift to heaven like the fluff of a dandelion in the wind. And then it will blossom in another garden, so bright the colors will hurt your eyes. That's how I imagined it. For Grandma, that's how I wanted it to be.

6

The Rifle

My sister Magda lived and breathed to caress her records. She was wild-eyed about them, and danger threatened anyone who touched even the most needle worn and milky surfaced. She had a stack as thick as an elephant's spine in the corner of her room, and copies, sometimes three, of her most precious favorites. She'd either slip them inside the flanges of a metal rack, or save them in a wooden box with a lever switch that locked with a miniature key.

On her wall, she thumbtacked magazine photos of her two dream stars, Elvis Presley and Smokey Robinson, surrounding them with a rainbow of paper colors. Elvis had a tough-guy sneer and tossed-back flame of black hair. Smokey had slit, romantic eyes. More than once I caught her drooping her head over them, dreaming.

The money for her records came from working at the Valley Laundry, a place she hated more than anything in the world. Her friend Linda said she was moody spirited and argued too much with the supervisor. Linda worked beside her on the steam press. She was in love with Nardo, but he didn't pay her any mind, mostly because blocks of fat sagged on her hips like a belt of thick Bibles, and she dressed in those elastic skirts, the kind with stretchy waists and no belt. Only with Linda, belts were the last worry, what with skin spilling out in all the worst places and buttons missing where you didn't want buttons missing.

Linda always showed wrinkles of concern over Magda, but when alone she confided to me that Magda had to learn how things worked at the laundry. You had to flirt a little with the supervisor. Pay attention to his lousy conversation. Flatter him a bit about his muscles. Two other flirty girls who worked there were already pushed over to Loading, and in another month they were going to push her over to Processing, but Magda's mouth was too smart-alecky for her own good, and the supervisor vowed he'd never in a million years move her up.

"Manny," Magda said, "that supervisor tells me I ain't doing the sheets right, that they ain't coming out of the machine right. Too many wrinkles. And I'm just sweating there, trying to do it right the best way I can. But you know, there ain't no *right* way of doing bedsheets. He just gets a big bang out of showing how he's got me under his thumb."

She was talking fast in front of her dresser mirror. She pressed a blunt pencil of mascara against her eyebrow, then picked up a tool shaped like a torture rack and stretched her eyelashes. She worked hard for beauty, teasing her hair high as an ocean wave, blushing pink on her cheeks and sometimes smearing her lips dark as pomegranate syrup. To me she was pretty enough with a naked face, but she never listened to me. Instead she bribed me when she wanted something. Like that day she promised me a cherry pie and a root beer.

"Keep an eye on Baby for a while, will you, Manny?" she begged, and just as quickly, hissed, "but don't say anything to Mom."

"Where're you going?"

"Out."

"Out where?"

"Out, out. That's all you need to know."

Magda bit at her pink-lacquered nails that she ate sometimes down to slivers. Even painted, her fingertips were scalded red and puss-y.

She had a secret boyfriend, and since Mom was at Grandma's putting things away, and Dad was again at Rico's, she got me to stay home and baby sit Pedi while she smooched with him over by the maple trees. If Mom found out she'd have fainted dead away; Dad would have boiled over faster than salted water.

Adjusting the belt of her skirt, Magda straightened her collar. "I'll be right back," she said.

I watched her walk out the screen door and cross the yard separating our house from the grove of maple trees. Her hips had a confident swing and her shoulders were proud and sassy. When she reached the edge of the grass, a guy in a T-shirt and jeans came out from behind a tree and stood watching her. He had blond hair sleeked back with pomade, except for one wave which veered over his face like a broken hinge. It was obvious he'd spruced himself up. His chin glowed with a fresh shave, and his shoes were mirror polished. They walked into the trees.

When I turned around, Pedi was sitting on the couch, smearing chocolate from a half-eaten candy bar all over her face. I really had to keep an eye on her. Usually, she wouldn't unglue from the hem of Magda's skirt unless given a candy.

Left alone, she'd tumble off the couch or reach for boiling water. The day before, I caught her rubbing a stick in her hands until she rasped a splinter. She also suffered from allergies, which Mom first thought were congestion and shoved steaming water under her nose to loosen her lungs. When that didn't help, a doctor stuck tiny needle pricks along her back. Each prick swelled red, which meant practically everything alive in the wind—pollen, grass, smoke, even certain siftings of dust—could bring tears and wheezing fits.

I took a chair from the kitchen and propped it on the door of Dad's closet, reaching far back into the shelf. I scraped my knuckle on the aimer of his rifle. He'd gotten it back from the police by spending a hundred and fifty dollars on a lawyer for a rifle that had cost fifty bucks. Mom said that was the stupidest thing she ever heard, but she didn't say anything to him about it.

With my finger, I traced a zero around the barrel hole, feeling the cold dead steel and imagining a bullet, tiny as a sliver, racing up my arm and zinging into my brain. I searched around some more and found what I was looking for, the box of dominoes.

"Come on, Pedi," I said, wiping chocolate from her face. "Let's build a house."

Most kids act like your fingers are made of hot glass when you touch them, but not Pedi. She liked people to wipe her face or squish the soft pillows of her arms. If you rubbed her head, she'd get drowsy and knock out in a minute.

I stood the dominoes up one by one. After settling Pedi's hands on her lap, I announced a *tah dah* and tapped the first domino. They collapsed in a riffling click of doom, but Pedi didn't notice the spectacle. At the last second she turned her head to the door, her eyes anxious for Magda's return.

"Come on now, Pedi," I pleaded, gathering the dominoes into a pile. "Look, let's build a house."

Pedi rose and climbed onto the couch. She stretched her neck in the direction Magda had gone, pressing her temple against the windowpane, her breath blurring a small balloon on the glass.

"Did she go to the store?"

"Yeah, she went to the store."

"Why'd she go to the store for?"

"She went to get some root beer." I noticed her dirt-black tennis shoes crushing smudges on the couch. "You know, Pedi, you shouldn't be stepping on the cushions. You know how Mom gets."

"There's root beer in the 'figerator."

"Not the kind that tastes like vanilla."

"Uh huh! There's that kind, too."

"Did I say vanilla? No, I meant chocolate."

"Chocolate?"

"Yeah, chocolate."

Pedi's eyes narrowed keen with suspicion. "You're lying, ain't you?" she said.

"Hey, I'm no liar."

"Yeah, you're a liar. A big fat *gordo* liar!"

"No I'm not," I said, although I could tell by her face that she knew I was lying.

Pedi slapped a hand on her pant leg and turned back to the window. When smaller, she was always arguing jibberish. Her speech was hard to understand, but you could tell when she was mad at you. She'd scrunch her face, and her fists would open and close with fury.

Usually, though, I had fun teasing her into tantrums, but only when Mom or Magda were around to quiet down her hysterics. Besides, at that moment, seeing her face empty of any trust in me didn't make me feel good about bothering her.

"Come on, Pedi," I said, "look, look at the house I built."

Actually, I was surprised myself, because without thinking, I had put together a three-story domino house. One piece remained to be put on top, and I was about to do it when Pedi climbed down off the couch.

"Hey, now, check this out," I coaxed. "It ain't even just any old house. It's a regular palace."

Avoiding my eyes, Pedi knelt on the floor, shuffling her knees closer. As she did, she placed her fist on the floor and pushed it forward. Before I could stop her, she bulldozed the domino house to rubble.

"Now, what did you do that for?!" I said, my voice lengthening into a whine.

She didn't say anything, only inched back a little on her knees. Instead of getting up, though, she suddenly splashed all the domino ruins across the floor. "Because you're a liar!"

There wasn't much to do after that. Afraid she'd start screeching, I quietly collected the dominoes and slipped them back into the cardboard box.

Sulking, her eyes squeezed shut, she sat back on the couch. I thought how Magda, if she were

97

there, would probably toss around pouty faces with her for hours. She liked to argue and back-bite with her, and laugh when Pedi pressed her hands to her sides in anger.

When I noticed her sneaking glances at me, measuring my patience, which by then I had to admit was pretty much punched out of air, I didn't even blink—blank was how I played it, blank. I just kept picking up the scattered dominoes like all I did my whole life was pick up dominoes. When I finished packing them in the box, I sat down opposite her on the couch.

After a while, she stood up, roughly tucking her T-shirt into her pants. Peering once at me with tight eyebrows, she looked down at the floppy laces of her tennis shoes and after another light-ning glance at me, knelt down to tie them. Then she went into the kitchen, sliding her chin haugh-tily over her shoulder.

I heard the refrigerator swoosh open and the crack of an ice tray. After what sounded like trouble reaching the faucet, she came to the door-way, a long plastic Tupperware cup in her hand. She sipped from the rim, watching me, shaking her head in little yeses and nos.

I answered her with a sizzling stare, then

turned quickly around, like the sight of her had offended my eyes.

After a while I felt a little tap on my head. When I turned around, Pedi nudged her forehead into my shoulder. She didn't say anything at first, only looped her wrist around my neck. "You're not a liar," she said, finally, in a forgiving voice.

"It's okay," I said, wiping my shirt. A small slink of snot had dripped from her nose onto my shirt.

After a while, Pedi fell asleep with her head cradled on my lap, but I eased out from under her and went back to the closet. I was curious about Dad's rifle. I wondered why he loved it so much, why he was willing to argue with the police over keeping it, and why he'd spend every cent we had in the bank plus what he could borrow to get it back. Then it was in my hands, and I began working the bolt arm as if inside were all the secrets.

Even then, it remained jammed. I began to work it, and suddenly it slid smooth and easy and I saw the round heel of a bullet rise and flutter a moment in the air, as if to pop out and fall on the floor, but instead it sank back into the chamber. Startled, I lifted my head, my eyes falling straight along the barrel, then on the aimer, and above it, Pedi, walking through the door, her tiny fists unscrewing sleep from her eyes.

The sound of the gun going off was like a huge mouth swallowing a noise, and Pedi was eaten by that mouth. Thoughts ran together inside my head and blurred, like currents of fast water flowing together. Loud shrieks inside my lungs were bursting to get out, but couldn't. Pedi was dead, I knew it. The way she fell back on the floor, she could only be dead. I was afraid to go up to her, thinking I'd see a gory gash where the bullet entered her head and I'd lose my mind.

My muscles felt weak and droopy. I thought I was going to pass out, but then I heard her crying, and when I speeded over to her, her mouth was fluttering. Tears sprouted from her eyes and leaked down past her ears, but this only made me laugh; my heart felt like it was being squeezed between two hands; joy and grief pressing and unpressing.

As she lay there on the floor, sucking air, I said, "Pedi, Pedi. Shhh, shhh!!!" My hands were jittering, as if tied to puppet strings, and my voice leaked through a wet sponge. I stopped to massage my cheeks, thawing them little by little.

If Mom had seen what happened, all the wrinkles on her face would have snapped shut. But she hadn't. No one had, not even Pedi, really. She hardly knew what happened.

I hid the rifle back in the closet right away, and after calming my mind down and staunching Pedi's crying, I put her back to sleep on the living room couch. That's when Magda came home. I turned on the TV fast and pretended to watch an old John Wayne movie.

Magda was glowing with perspiration and breathing in little gulps of air when she walked through the door. She took off her earrings and looked at me. Her hair was mashed down in the back and she was trying to fluff it with her fingers. "Did anybody come?"

"No."

"What about Pedi, did she cry?"

"No."

The TV was buzzing a loud, comforting current of electricity. Magda tilted her head around in a swivel, dabbing at stray hair. She went over to the TV and turned it off just as John Wayne, in the midst of squiggles, was dying on a bulldozer. The humming stopped, but the sound buzzed in the air before the current finally died away. "What was that noise a little while ago?" she asked.

"Why's your hair all messed up?"

"Well, not that it's any of your business, but there's a lot of wind out there you know."

"Oh yeah?"

"Yeah!" She pursed her lips and tugged menacingly at a tuft of my hair. "If you're thinking of telling any lies to Mom about me, you better think again." She gave my hair a yank and held on with a twisting pinch. "Do you *hear* me!?"

"Hear what?" Mom said, coming in through the door. She had a bag of groceries under her arm. "Did he hear what?"

Magda quickly let go my hair. Seeing her dressed like she was, and me with my face rubbery, Mom was suspicious.

"Nothing's going on, Mom. Manny's just being a pest, that's all," she said, sidling up against me. She wanted me to know that she'd give me pain if I spilled my guts.

Mom put the bag of groceries down on the glass-top table. "What's really going on here?"

Just then Pedi woke up, her eyes drowsy and focusing. I felt a heavy pressing on my chest. When she saw Mom, she crawled across the couch and clamped her arms around her waist. "Mama . . . you know what? Manny . . ."

"Wait a minute, *mija*." Mom said, hoisting her up by the armpits and sitting her back on the couch. Not altogether awake, Pedi flopped back asleep. Mom looked about the room like small flames were beginning to sprout on the floor. "What the hell is going *on* here, Magda? Why are you dressed up like that? Did anybody come?"

"Nobody came, Momma," Magda said, dryly.

"Then why are you dressed up like that?"

"I'm just trying on new clothes for tomorrow, that's all. We're supposed to go to work dressed up sometimes."

"You never dressed up for work before."

"Yeah, I have. I've gone to work dressed up!"

"No, never." Mom sounded sure, but also a touch disappointed that she'd caught Magda in a lie. She never scolded her, since she was too grown up and the only one in the family working steady.

"I've dressed up before," Magda said, glancing at me. She expected a nod of agreement, but I didn't give her one. She pursed her lips and twirled back with an innocent smile. "How's Grandma's house? Is Dad still going to sell it?"

103

About to open her mouth to answer, Mom instead curled her finger slowly, as if trying to pluck something delicate out of the air. "Don't make the same mistake I did, Magdalena," she said. "Don't ruin your life, *mija.*"

"I'm not ruining my life, Mom! You keep saying I'm going to ruin my life."

Mom shook her head like she wasn't listening. She'd gathered up her own thoughts, and would use *them* to do the figuring. "Your father and I ran off together when I was sixteen. You were already big in my belly." For a moment she looked to put her hand on Magda's shoulder, but held back, rubbing her arms. "Don't make the same mistake I did, that's all I have to say."

At first Magda said nothing. If she'd kept quiet everything might have blown over. But then an angry heat began seeping into her face. She could understand Mom being angry at her. She could accept any punishment, but she couldn't accept the fact that she'd already been judged— especially in the voice Mom used, a voice like an accusing needle—and there was nothing left for her to do but be guilty.

Magda, breathing heavily, pinched her eyelids tight. "You don't tell me what to do," she said, in an even voice, but squeezing her fists. Then she widened her mouth. "You shouldn't *ever* tell me what to do!"

"I'm not telling you what to do!" Mom said, surprised by her sudden anger.

"Yes, you are . . . you are," Magda said, unclamping one finger from her starchy knuckles. "If you ever tell me about my business again I'm going to leave. You hear me!? Me and Linda, we'll get our own place. What will you do then, huh, Mom, with no money? What will you do then?"

Mom looked like she'd been poked in the chest with an icepick. She stammered. There was a squeak in her voice. *"Mija,* I only . . ."

Her voice sparked a watery trickle in my throat, but there was nothing I could do. When Mom and Magda warred against each other, it was their war, and anyone who got in between them became an enemy. Magda's face was fierce, and loaded with hurt. She braced her legs and wiped a splash of spit from the side of her twisted mouth. Whatever scolding or advice Mom had once been able to give her, she wasn't going to take anymore.

That's when Mom's eyes began to weaken, and she bent down slowly to pick up the groceries from the glass-top table. She walked into the kitchen and set the bag rustling on the linoleum counter. It tipped over, and a can of pork and beans rolled out, stopping on the metal flange of the counter and bobbing back. Mom watched it, then turned to open the closet door next to the pantry. She grabbed a broom, shrugged, and began sweeping, the straw bristles scraping the floor. First one corner then another, she herded the dirt to the center of the room.

I pulled out a bedsheet from the hamper, and for the rest of the afternoon lay down in the hallway underneath the water cooler, relieved that Mom hadn't found out about me almost shooting Pedi. I crunched lightning out of ice cubes and watched the sun slowly whittle away the shadows from the walls. The sun, pressing down on everything, was too crippling to let anyone do anything other than drag oneself around. In that heat even the birds squirmed, and if you stood in the sun, it was like your shadow was groaning to escape.

My mother kept coming in and telling me to get out of her way. Once to bring in chairs from the kitchen, while she mopped the floor, another time to string a clothesline from one end of the hallway to the other. Water swished in the kitchen sink as she squeezed clothes against the scrubboard, churning, then wracking and splatting them as she ruffled the wetness out.

"Mom, how're those gonna dry under the cooler?" I asked, raising up on my elbow.

"Oh, they'll dry. Don't you worry about that. In this heat even ice will dry. Besides, you don't have to worry, the cooler's going off."

"Off!"

"Yes, off!" she said, shoving me with her foot. "Do you think electricity is free?"

She didn't turn off the cooler, though. Her hand paused over the switch, and she sort of half turned her head toward me. Then she bustled back into the kitchen.

I don't know how long I lay there not thinking anything, watching the clothes flutter under the cooler breeze. I saw one of Magda's dresses hanging above me on the clothesline, a flower print with fluffy shoulders and gardenia patterns stitched on the bottom hem. I saw Nardo's white shirt that he used when he was a busboy, with ghosts of smudges on it. Whenever he sprouted beyond his sleeve size, Mom trimmed his clothes and passed them down to me.

107

Then I began thinking about a lot of things. I thought about this girl in school, Maria, how she sat behind me in class and I could feel her breath on my neck, smelling of caramel candy. The way her hair was soft around her ears made my stomach landslide with a strange, delirious emotion. For a long time, I remember, I couldn't touch anything without feeling a little current of mystery traveling inside it.

All my thoughts were coming forward, one by one, then flying away. I thought about the time in spring, after the rains came and everything sighed, how I climbed the largest maple in the Big Lawn and looked around. I could see people walking under me, hear their voices, as I lazily veered on the branches, the wind twittering the leaves. I thought about Nardo, who was hardly ever home anymore. Always on the move, drinking with his wino friends, snatching up his coat while feeding a long line of excuses to Mom's disbelieving ears. I thought about how Mom kept cleaning the house, shifting dirt from one place to another. Maybe she thought she could get the house so spanking shiny that someday it'd disappear in one great sparkle, and she'd be free. I thought about Dad, how on his breezier days, he'd unhook the buttons on his sleeve and fix something around the house. When was he going to quit butting his head against a wall? When was he either going to break it, or break his head? I thought about happy times, too. I thought about Grandma; how when she got new eyeglasses, she discovered Mexican movies. She liked to see the singer Flor Silvestre cradled in her costumes of spun radiance, and watch westerns from Mexico, with brick-red sunsets and a ribbon of blue mountains in the distance.

For a long time I lay there, thinking, my head pillowed on my arm. Thoughts came like damp, echoing coughs, and the air felt empty. I sort of began to feel like no gravity was holding me, and I was spiraling down a long, black tunnel. Looking up, I remembered the bullet, which I figured got buried inside the cooler shaft. I prayed no one would ever see it. The thought of how close I'd come to killing Pedi gave my lungs a peculiar sponginess, as if apart from my body they'd been sobbing for hours.

7

The Boxing Match

hen summer ended, I was again at the same school. Mom's plans to get me transferred didn't work out. The administration said it was too late. There were already too many kids in that school. There was an imbalance in the student body—whatever that meant. They said lots of things, but it all ended with me not transferring.

So I was sitting with my friend Albert Sosa, eating lunch on the picnic table over by the maple trees, when all of a sudden Lencho Dominguez came and parked his big beefy shadow above us. We liked eating lunch there, because every day around twelve o'clock one of the English teachers, Miss Van der Meer, would step out of her class-room and swoon our minds with the gorgeous way she'd fluff her hair and fix the collar of her ruffly blouse. Her legs dangled from the hem of her skirt like two shapely white bowling pins, and her shoulders were straight as a geography book.

We acted like that wasn't why we ate lunch

there, but it was. Anybody could see how cold it got. The wind already had glass edges to it, stiffening muscles and practically cutting through the stitches of our clothes. When it blew, the chill stabbed our teeth like icicles, and our voices jiggled every time we talked. Yet our eyes melted when Miss Van der Meer appeared at the door.

Anyway, Lencho came over and eyed us like we were hopeless. He was dressed in Big Ben pants, starched stiff as ironing-boards, and a plaid Pendleton shirt with the lap and tail out. Hardly a smile of a wrinkle showed anywhere. He cleared his throat with an exaggerated gutter.

"You *vatos* are real screwy, you know that?" he said, in his strep-throaty voice.

Rumor had it that Lencho stripped his voice by smoking cartons of Lucky Strike cigarettes and drinking Jack Daniel's whisky straight from a thermos bottle stashed in his locker. He leaned over and fingered about a dozen of Albert's fried potatoes. "That white bitch teaches a class of *gavachos*, and you guys hang around waiting to see her ass."

"Whataya mean?" Albert said, acting sore about Lencho thieving his potatoes. He knew better than to complain, though. No one complained to

111

Lencho. I once saw him grab Mark Calavasos by the tits and squeeze until he grit his teeth and begged Lencho to please, please let him go.

"You guys ever been in that room?" Lencho mumbled, snatching and pushing another load of Albert's potatoes into his mouth.

"No," I said, pretending to not be interested. Actually, I must have wondered a thousand times about what was behind that door.

Daintily flicking salt from his fingers, Lencho did a curious thing. He wet his two fingers on his tongue, and pinching the crease of his pants, ran them down to his knee. He did the same with the other pant leg. We watched him with open-mouthed fascination.

"Well, let me tell you *vatos*," he said, finishing his grooming with a swipe of his pocket. "There's couches and sofas in there. You guys ever seen couches and sofas in a *class*room?" He laughed, a sort of half chuckle, half sneering laugh. We looked dumbly at him, and he laughed again, only louder. "You *vatos* are screwy—you know that? You're a couple of real sissies."

He didn't say it like an insult, but more a statement of fact. If he'd have asked us, we'd have agreed with him in a second. Compared to

Lencho, *everybody* was a sissy. He had lumpy sacks of potatoes for shoulders, and even the weight of his breathing made you feel puny.

He put his knuckle to his mouth and cleared a big wad of phlegm and spat it out. "I want to talk to you about something, Manny," he said, seriously. "Do you think that maybe Bernardo might wanna join my boxing team?"

"I don't know," I said.

"He's a pretty tough *vato*, ain't he?"

"I guess so."

"What do you mean you *guess* so? Don't you know anything about your own brother?"

"He doesn't tell me everything!" I said, trying to toughen my voice. I must have sounded whiny, though, because Albert ducked his eyes.

It was the truth about Nardo. He mostly told me what he had done and how he felt about what he had done, but never anything about what he was planning to do or anything about what he wanted to do. If he thought about something, he'd ask me in a question, like, 'Hey, Manny, do you think I should join Lencho's boxing team?' He hadn't asked me a thing like that lately, so I didn't know.

"Well, anyway, ask your brother if he wants to

113

join," Lencho said. He stamped his Stacy Adams shoes on the bench and walked away, eyeing his snazzy polish.

That's when Miss Van der Meer came out of her classroom. She had a load of books crooked under her arm and was mangling a cluster of keys against her hip. As usual, there were some white students pattering like puppies behind her. She fished a key out and locked the door. Lencho walked toward her, tiptoeing—with dignity— trying not to get any grass on his shoes. He hopped on the concrete walkway.

"Hey, Lench!" I yelled. "Albert says he wants to join. He says he could whip anybody in the whole school—even Boise. He says he'll even take on Boise." I got up and gave Albert's shoulders a champion's massage.

Annoyed, but not wanting to make a big commotion around a teacher, Lencho turned and shot a hidden Screw You finger at me from his hip; then, coolly deadening his face, he zipped past Miss Van der Meer, almost bumping her shoulder.

As he passed, the white students cold-stared Lencho like he'd just peed on the Queen of England. They weren't about to say anything, though. They knew his reputation. Besides, Miss

Van der Meer pretended like she hadn't noticed a thing. That's the kind of teacher she was, too precious to notice anything.

That's when I yelled out, "Hi, Miss Van der Meer!" It was one of those phony-baloney hi's that always comes out sounding smoochy. She turned around and automatically started to wave back, but then recognized that she didn't know who I was. She tossed a polite hand at me anyway, and her students hurried her away.

"You jerk! What the hell you do that for?" Albert moaned after Miss Van der Meer and her pack of puppies rounded the corner. He was steamed. He snatched angrily at his hair. He stood up, grabbed his books like he was about to huff off, then changed his mind and plunked them back down on the table. "Man," he said, in a mopey voice, "now she's gonna think we're a coupla idiots."

"We *are* a coupla idiots, you idiot," I said, defiantly, but I could see regret tightening on Albert's face. He was convinced that we'd never get another chance to moon over Miss Van der Meer on the sly. But to me, Lencho was right. It was stupid sitting out there stuffed in a mountain of double sweaters, waiting for some teacher to make a grand appearance. She paid us less mind than she would a wad of chewing gum stuck on the sidewalk. That much I could tell by the way she waved at me.

I wanted to tell Albert this, but he was looking like he just got plugged on the shoulder with an arrow. "Man, Lencho's gonna have it *in* for you!" he said finally, perking up in almost a gleeful way, like he wouldn't be *too* sorry if Lencho knocked in my teeth.

"He won't do anything," I said.

"Oh, no!?" Albert stressed, anxious to prove me wrong.

"No," I said. "He doesn't want to mess with Nardo."

"Oh, yeah."

He was glum again. He didn't have a brother, only a sister, and she'd as soon slap him in the face as smile. When you're like Albert, and you don't have protection, any day of the week, on any street corner, a guy like Lencho can kick in your rib cage and nobody would give a damn.

All in all, I thought it amazing that Lencho even *tried* to spark up the Chicano guys to join his boxing team. Not that the Chicano guys couldn't fight or anything. There were a lot of ornery *vatos* around, but they just hung around and smoked and ditched class and acted like the school was some kind of contaminated nuclear zone. They'd never join any team that wasn't a gang.

Lencho did recruit two suckers, though. One was a guy named Chico. A nice guy, but as my brother Nardo once said about him, the only shining he ever did came from his teeth. He could draw a neat picture of a naked girl and follow the numbers in a bingo game, but putting his finger on an algebra problem would probably burn him to ashes. Chico once tried out for the basketball team, but he was too short and couldn't dribble to save his life. When scratched from the roster, he blamed Coach Rogers, the basketball and boxing coach. The coach wore tortoise-shell glasses and talked in a Marine voice. He had a head that reflected the sun and a blue-black carpet of hair over his muscular arms. Where Chico got the story, I don't know, but he said the coach once caught a Mexican guy frisking around with his daughter and ever since then he didn't like Mexican guys.

The other fish Lencho hooked—and no one

could believe it at first, especially me—was "Skinny Boy" Albert Sosa, my friend. I thought this was a pretty sorry thing for Lencho to do, considering Albert couldn't punch the air out of a soap bubble. Of course, it was a robustly stupid thing for Albert to do, too, since teachers lifted their eyebrows with appreciation when handing back his test papers.

But Albert wanted to show something about himself. He wanted to impress his dad maybe, who sat around watching TV all day, making fun of the white actors, or maybe he wanted to impress Miss Van der Meer, who you could tell sent fingers of ice down his neck.

I tried warning him. I tried explaining how ribs crack easy as dry twigs, and how a punch sometimes welcomes paralysis. But he wouldn't listen. He practically begged to sign up, and you could tell Lencho was disappointed at such a scrawny catch. He wanted guys like Nardo and Sammy Fuentes—dangers known to everyone.

But I think it was enough for Lencho to know that Chico and Albert would yank in whatever direction he pulled. They hung on his every word, and he could sure pump guys up with confidence. He belonged to this group called the Berets; older guys, mostly, already out of school. Actually, Lencho was only a Junior Beret, him still being in school and all. But to him, being a Junior Beret was still halfway better than a plain nobody.

The Berets believed that white people were our worst enemy, and if they had one purpose in mind, it was to keep brown people down. We, on the other hand, were descendants of Indians blessed with a color that was as necessary as dirt to the earth, as important as the sun to all the trees. We had treasures buried deep inside our blood, hidden treasures we hardly knew existed.

This is the kind of stuff I listened to from Lencho, who figured if he made me his equipment manager and handler, then maybe Nardo might change his mind and put on the leather.

For three weeks, I hung out with the boxers. Training was held after school in the weight room, where the guys bounced around swiveling their necks, skipping rope and running in place until wet as fish. Then, with faces swelling, they'd groan out a few dozen sit-ups. (Lencho didn't let them lift iron because he said weights make muscles bulky, and they needed to be quick and springy in the exchanges.)

For equipment, we had an old, hobo-looking

punching bag and one of those rubber tetherballs suspended on a bungee cord. On the first day, Albert hit the ball with a left, then came over— or *tried* to come over—with a right. The ball snapped back in a wobble and the cord gashed his fist. Between his two big knuckles, a flap of skin the size of a postage stamp opened a jagged eye.

Unwinding a jump rope in his hand, Lencho told him to skip the day's training, but to stick around for the pep talk. He didn't mean that, of course. What he really meant to say was that Albert should show his fireball commitment by toughing it out. He didn't say this, exactly; Lencho never said anything, exactly. Instead, he coolly started jumping rope and talking about how *real* fighters never let little chicken stuff like cuts put the coward's bite on them. After a long stare at the blood creeping under the Band-Aid he'd put on, Albert wrapped his hand in a T-shirt and began shuffling his feet around, jabbing at the air.

One of the fighters in Coach Rogers's stable was a black guy named Boise Johnson. During training Lencho took particular attention to stink up his name. Clapping his hands, he'd roughen his voice and say we were going to pluck him like a chicken, crush him like a pasta shell. These put-downs were meant to lift the guys' confidence, but both Chico and Albert blessed their skinny bones they weren't going to fight Boise.

There was also a feud going on between Lencho and Coach Rogers. The coach didn't appreciate him mavericking fighters on his own. He was a former Golden Gloves boxing champion, and he considered that a big deal. I think every student at J. Edgar Hoover High knew the coach was a Golden Gloves boxing champion. Even in junior high I remember knowing, and I think even my dad knew, and my dad didn't give a rat's ass about anything that happened in my school.

Coach Rogers selected his fighters from those who scored highest on the school's physical exams, which included climbing the high rope and squat-jumping and running windsprints until our lungs collapsed; but he depended, mostly, on who could lift the heaviest weights, or repeat the lighter weights the longest. This torture of selection dragged on for about two weeks, after which the guys who scored Excellent were given free gold trunks to wear and were invited later to join the football, basketball and boxing teams. The guys who scored Average could buy purple trunks

121

with silver trim to announce their standing. Those who scored Poor, like me, had to wear those gray gym trunks like a flag of shame.

What mostly fired us up, though, was Lencho's inspirational talks. He spoke with braids of lightning in his voice, saying stuff he'd learned in the Berets about Mexicans and Chicanos being a special people, how power slept in our fists and we could awaken it with a simple nod of our heroic will. He piled it on about being proud, about how marvelous it was going to be after we pulverized those other guys. Lencho could really swell the chest muscles.

After a couple of weeks of watching punches pop deeper into the bag, and guys skip blurs on the jump rope—Albert actually hit the tetherball four swipes in a row!—I began to get a little swell-headed about our chances. Sure, at first I was a bit leery, since those other guys were bigger and could cross their arms when jumping rope, but they weren't any better than us, not really.

One day, while walking over by B Hall, I was surprised to hear my name called from behind. "Oh, Manuel! Manuel!"

It was Miss Van der Meer, bustling over, a pile

of books shoved up against her breasts. She was walking in that cute, pigeon-toed way that used to make Albert and me do crazy rolls with our eyes.

"Do you think Leonard will win the contest?" she asked, stopping in front of me. She began to busily shuffle the order of her books on her chest.

"Yeah, I guess so," I said. "He's pretty confident."

"Yes, I noticed that about him," she said, waving her finger in the air. "He's a regular Hotspur."

"A hot what?" I asked. I thought maybe she was talking about some kind of bullsticker or thorn.

"Hotspur, in Shakespeare, you know."

I must have looked blank, because she got this disappointed frown on her face.

"Well, it's not important," she said, matter-of-factly. Her face was sprayed with sun freckles, and with her finger she delicately crooked back her bangs. She was beautiful, with swirls of glowing sunlight floating on her hair.

I was going to grab her free hand and shake it, but she started fiddling with the bindings of her books.

"Anyway," she said, "you tell Leonard for me that I wish him all the luck in the world. Will you do that, Manuel?" She made her hand straight as a Ping-Pong paddle and patted me a couple of times on the shoulder.

My heart lumped in my throat, and when I said, "Yeah, sure, Miss Van der Meer," my voice was thick as oatmeal.

Of course I didn't tell Lencho anything. He'd probably have spit at my shoes and said, *What a bitch!* He'd probably say something nasty, too, like why was a dog like me still sniffing after her tail. He talked like that sometimes when he wasn't getting all glorious about the Mexican race.

Not until Miss Van der Meer walked away did I wonder how she knew my name. I figured she must have asked someone, or looked it up in the administration files. Whichever way, I could tell by her eyes that she knew something about me. But then, I'd found out some things about her, too. For one, she wasn't one of the regular teachers, but a sort of extra teacher for the white students bussed in from Alemany High. I also found out about the couches and sofas in her classroom, because I asked the janitor, an El Salvadoran man who once worked with my dad in the onion fields. He scratched the back of his neck, and said, *"O sí, allí tienen sofás, lámparas y todo.*" He thought it was a teachers' lounge.

What all this has to do with the fight, I don't know. Usually I didn't like thoughts about teachers browsing around inside my head, but Miss Van der Meer was special. I hoped, in fact, that by some wildcard of luck they'd transfer me over from Mr. Shattler's class, where all we did was read magazines and play bingo games, to hers, where students read detective books and stuff by that Shakespeare guy. Except for Albert, the guys I hung with thought that if they even flicked through the pages of a book, ink would rub off on their hands and mark them sissies for life. I could imagine them in a classroom like Miss Van der Meer's, getting all cushy on the couches; throwing spit-wads at her butt.

The boxing tournament was announced in every home room in the school, and on flyers stapled in the hallways. Hardly a word passed across anyone's lips that didn't include the thrill they *hoped* they'd get when somebody got knocked out cold.

Being an official trainer, I got a reputation among a couple of girls, Rachel and Mary, who hung over by the baseball diamond. Their attitudes toward me couldn't have changed more completely. They said hi to me now, whereas before I would've died if just one of them had thrown me her eyes.

The day of the tournament, the basketball gym was packed from hoop to hoop. Waves of nervous anticipation washed like an ocean surf across the bleachers, and there was barely standing room by the push-open doors, where it was so pressed no one dared breathe.

The boxing ring was four brass stands taken from the school auditorium, linked by a long, furry velvet rope. They were just for show. A fighter would have to be crazy to lean against those ropes. The actual ring was a square of thick brown masking tape in the center of a huge wrestling mat.

Lencho invited his cronies from the Berets to come witness his spectacle. Decked out in khaki shirts and brown beret hats, their shoes polished to a smooth military sheen, they stood over by the exit doors intimidating anyone who happened to walk into their space. I was surprised to see Miss Van der Meer there, trying not to look excited. Old Mr. Hart, my history teacher, was there too, pacing on the sidelines and bogusly snuffling his nose with a crumpled handkerchief. Being the timekeeper and bell ringer, he was sweating diamonds.

I waited at ringside. I saw Nardo pump a fist at me as he and his friends Felix Contreras and Johnny Martinez crowded their way to a middle bleacher. He called to me, but I couldn't hear. The noise in the gym sounded warped, like a blackboard bending, about to splinter and crack. Blood hissed along my temples and my earlobes pulsed like tiny engines. *This is the biggest moment of my life,* I thought.

I was supposed to get the ring corner organized, so I gave everything an anxious onceover; Lencho didn't want to be bothered by details. I had gym towels, water bottles, an already melting ice pack stuffed in a plastic bucket, and three mouthpieces wrapped in a clean white handkerchief. I had tape and Vaseline and those stretch wraps used for sprained ankles, although what I'd actually use them for was a mystery. The Berets paid for all the equipment, so I'd grabbed everything on the shelf.

The first fight was Albert's. He was to take on Boise's brother, Rochel Johnson, and from the look of Roach's arms, I knew somebody didn't

127

keep an eye on the weight scales. Albert, if he breathed deep, probably weighed no more than an ounce above a hundred and nine pounds. Rochel looked, not a little, but a lot heavier.

I saw worry leaking out of Lencho's face. Unfortunately, Albert saw this too, because he stared at Rochel like he was Godzilla about to trample over Tokyo.

The fight was lopsided from the beginning, and lasted only about two minutes, although for me it was a hundred and twenty long, painfully slow seconds. Albert kept backing away and backing away until the crowd started whistling. The whistling soon turned to jeering and the jeering into sneering disgust. But that was okay, since the sneers shrunk the noise down enough for Lencho to holler, "Throw a combination! Throw a combination!" He punched his fists in the air to demonstrate, but Albert just looked at him like he'd been slapped on the face with a wet towel. "Charge, then, goddam it. Charge!" Lencho urged.

Unfortunately, Albert charged. But Rochel saw him coming from a mile away, and with his gloves up and head leaning to one side he moved smartly out of the way. Albert stumbled past him, tripped and smacked his nose on one of the auditorium stands. Everybody oohhed and awwhed and mangled their collars like it was them that got their noses smashed. Coach Mazzini mercifully waved the fight over.

Albert's face was awful with defeat; Lencho's was a torment of disappointment. He stuffed some ice in a towel and roughly pinched Albert's nose shut. The nosebleed bloomed a rose of blood in the towel, and Albert started to cry in wet, little puppy whimpers. Lencho, with a sigh, told me to grab the towel and take him into the locker room.

That sure was a mistake. I knew it as soon as I walked into the locker room because there, dressing for his fight, was Chico—late as usual. Before I could tell him it was just a plain bloody nose, Chico took one look at the blood sopping the towel, and his face glazed over with shock.

"Hey, it's okay," I said, reassuringly. I left Albert by his locker. "It's only a bloody nose."

"Only a bloody nose!" Chico cried, clutching at his hair. He was stiff with panic. If somebody at that moment had pushed him over, he'd have landed flat on the back of his head.

I tried to grab his arm and lead him into the

gym, but he shrugged me off and walked like a zombie down the locker aisle. I was afraid he'd suddenly bolt for the exit doors. *Oh no,* I said to myself. *What am I going to do?* I ran down the aisle and grabbed him by the shoulder.

"Hey, you're not *scared,* are you?" I said, trying to be peppy.

Chico stared blank at me for a while, then a little spark of embarrassment flashed in his eyes. "Hell, no, I was just, I was just going to get my towel."

"No, no," I insisted, "I got towels, I got plenty of towels! Hey man," I said with exaggerated pride, "I came *prepared!*"

This seemed to boost Chico's spirit a little, and he let me steer him through the swinging rubber doors and into the gym.

As soon as Chico and I walked in, a stampede began in the bleachers. The Mexicans, both guys and girls, began hammering the floorboards and hooting like wild Yaquis. It was a big cheer, considering the school was mostly black, with a few whites bussed in from across town.

When Chico and I reached the corner, Lencho was clapping these hard, buffeting claps, like he was a thousand times relieved to see us. He practically popped the knuckles out of my hand when he grabbed it.

I looked over and saw Nardo jamming his arm in the air, and could hear Rachel and Mary screeching Chico's and my names. The girlish pitch of their voices sliced through the noise like a paper cut. It touched down softly on my heart and opened a tiny slit that spilled sweet and aching all around inside me.

Lencho hurriedly sat Chico on the stool. "You hear that?" he said, stoking his courage. "That's for you! That's so you can show this guy who the real man is. Now, don't let your *Raza* down."

I left off listening and glanced about hoping to spot Rachel or Mary. I saw them, hair teased high and stiff, excitedly smacking their lips and rolling gum over their teeth. I saw Nardo again, too, standing on the bleachers. He was winding his shoulders as if readying to fight himself. Feeling proud and nervous at the same time, I flipped the towel over my shoulder, but it landed on the floor.

Lencho had revved Chico up. When the bell rang, he shot off his stool like a man in a desperate search for dropped money. He started punching at the guy, aiming for his stomach, but mostly hitting arms and shoulders.

The guy Chico fought was Malcolm Augustus, who was now in my biology class. He was the only one in the whole class who knew the answer to the teacher's question about how much blood spills when a girl's on her period. Guys were saying a gallon and girls were acting like they knew it already, but nobody really knew—except Malcolm, who said it was about six tablespoons. Imagine, six tablespoons!

Surprised at first by Chico's aggressiveness, Malcolm soon calmed down and stabbed him with some head jabs. When Chico ducked low to avoid getting his head snapped back, Malcolm unhinged an uppercut right under his chin. Chico stumbled back, looking like he'd stuck a fork into a light socket. I thought, *Oh no, we're doomed!* But Chico sparked up again and in a flutter of blows drove Malcolm outside the ring tape.

"You see that, did you see that uppercut!" Lencho shouted when Chico stumbled back to the corner. "That was the stupidest move the *vato* could've done. When he does that, just ignore it and come over the top with a left hook. You'll knock him out, I'm not kidding, you'll knock him out!" Lencho grabbed one of the bottles from my hand and splashed water on Chico's face. He fumbled when handing the bottle back and clunked me on the forehead. "Now, I want you to body punch that bastard until he squirms," he said, turning to Chico again, "and remember, remember the left hook!"

Chico didn't remember the left hook. He couldn't have remembered his name if you asked him. Halfway through the round his legs were making wobbly journeys around the ring. He did toss some slaps and chicken-wing flutters, but at the end of the second round he looked so winded you couldn't have put a baby to sleep in his arms.

In the third round Chico tried to duck a jab and come inside, but instead ran smack into Malcolm's elbow, and was knocked out cold. They had to carry him out flat on a blanket. People's eyes widened as they took him out the exit doors. His own eyes were ditched back inside his head, and he was slobbering all over one of the blanket carrier's hands. A smart aleck from the rafters yelled out, "Emergency! Emergency!" That got a big laugh from everybody, except Coach Rogers, who shoved his way up the bleachers and gave the guy the heave-ho out of the gym.

Right away talk turned to Boise and Lencho. All the excitement became sharp as a cone.

What happened first, though, was that the leader from the Berets, a guy named Miguel, wearing a cadet's starched khaki uniform, took over my job at the corner just as I was putting Lencho's gloves on. "Take a seat, Ace," he said, and without so much as an Excuse Me, he swished the towel off my shoulder and draped it over his own.

I tried to say something in Lencho's ear about uppercuts and strategy, but Miguel pushed me away. Lencho was too nervous to listen, anyway. And no wonder. Miguel right away started nudging him on the ribs, nodding up, and reminding him how many people were in the audience. Lencho's face wrung stiff as a twisted rope.

In the other corner, Coach Rogers and Boise seemed like two cozy sweet potatoes in the dirt. Boise's face was smooth from his warm-up, dark and shiny, like an icy glass of Coca-Cola. He wasn't wearing a shirt, and a tiny sapphire necklace of sweat strung across his lean belly. Just another fight to old Boise, I thought. Cool, that's what he was, cool, with nothing jumping around in his face and nobody in his corner giving him the jitters.

Lencho and Boise being about the same size, and the two guys in the school whose muscles were the most crowded together, it was natural that people would get excited about pitting them against each other. Seeing Lencho, proud and ready for action, you couldn't help but back him. And then there was Boise. He didn't strain against the threads of his clothes like Lencho, but he was what everybody in the Boys' Gym called "ribbed." He even looked like a boxer, his nose square and puffy around the eyes, like he'd just awakened from a dream of beating up people.

The referee was Coach Mazzini. He had this big watersack gut that got in the way of everything, but otherwise he knew what to do, which was mostly to keep fighters from chickening out of the ring. When Mr. Hart clanged the bell announcing the start of the fight, everyone screwed their butts tight to their seat.

After a moment of staring at each other hard enough to shove a crowbar across a table, Lencho right away began wrenching left hooks and long winding right crosses; Boise ducked and uppercutted to the body. It was a mean fight, a blur that even if you slowed it down by half, it would still be a blur. Even Coach Mazzini, fat belly and all, sprinted out of the ring and didn't go back in until Mr. Hart smacked the bell ending the first round.

The whole gym busted open with screams and foot stomping that almost brought the bleachers crashing down. Lencho came back to the corner, breathing huge and proud in his sweaty T-shirt, a fat grin on his face.

In the bleachers, it was a circus. Guys were dancing and girls collapsing over each other. The girls pawed over the guys and the guys pretended to hug them as they fainted on their laps. But then needling stuff, like arguing and weasely bragging, sparked between some black and brown guys. A few even began to shove each other and spit into arguments. Then the bell to the second round clanged and everybody right away sat down.

Boise was still calm, a gob of Vaseline dangling on his chin. At first he'd dip his shoulder and ease over to the side when Lencho charged. Then he began grinding punches into Lencho's belly, and suddenly, like a tidal wave, rise up to hammer him on the side of the head. A queery smile smeared across Lencho's face a couple of times.

That's when he began to shy away, stirring his gloves in the air like he was waving away flies. To show he wasn't stunned when he came back to the corner, he sunk his lips into a confident smirk. You could tell, though, that this was a sloppy excuse. In the bleachers, it was so quiet you could practically hear people breathing.

Whatever Lencho's plans were for the third round, they weren't very good. Boise began laying up for him, butting him on the jaw with jabs and swinging catapult blows against his ribs, making him grunt deep. To protect himself, Lencho crossed his arms and began stepping back, stubbornly jerking his chin from side to side to avoid blows. When Boise sledgehammered him on the side of the ear, his shoulders stiffened and his jaw squinched like a little electricity had run through it.

My heart was jerking around inside my chest, I was so nervous. My eyelashes were tiny wings beating in a fevery air, yet my face felt frozen, as if blasted by an arctic wind. I couldn't tell if my mouth was smiling or grinning.

Lencho didn't even bother coming in anymore, but just stood there gritting tighter on his mouthpiece, following Boise around the ring with beaten eyes. You could tell then that he was finished.

I pressed the sides of my cheeks to settle the nerves down, but my face kept on jumbling. Miguel, beside me, was yelling for Lencho to go forward. "Come on, Lencho! Come on! Attack! Attack!"

I felt like screaming for him to shut up. The truth was, I was afraid that Lencho would go down. If he did, I didn't know what I'd do. I had expected and wanted so much from him, that for him to disappoint me then would hurt, really hurt. I suddenly realized that the whole fight shouldn't have been given so much meaning. When pumped up with pride, something so ugly as a boxing match could only grow too cruel to maintain; it could only burst, right in everybody's faces.

When old Mr. Hart finally clanged the bell, ending the fight, I was relieved. It was obvious who had won. Coach Rogers gave Boise a big bear hug of victory. Then he rushed over and—real corny!—like he really meant it, cupped Lencho behind the neck like a proud father, staring into his eyes.

Miguel left the ringside in a hurry to talk with the Beret guys standing over by the exit doors. You could see their faces had hardened against showing what they really felt. Later, when it was all over, after they had *analyzed* it and all, they decided to kick Lencho out of the Berets. They said that he brought embarrassment to them, and worse, caused a loss of unity between them and their black brothers.

But that was later. Right then no one was around, except me, and Lencho kept searching for somebody to take off his gloves. Even when Boise came over—his own gloves off and, with his two naked hands, shook Lencho's arms—Lencho looked down at his gloves sort of funny, the way you look at a dog that has just dug up your garden, halfway angry at the dog and halfway sad about the garden. A hunk of concrete weighed on my chest and gopher teeth were gnawing at my heart, but I went over and began peeling the tape and undoing the laces—because Lencho wanted somebody to take off his gloves.

■8■

Family Affair

The day we took Magda to the hospital, the wind against my ears sounded like sizzling, it was so cold. I remember tears of ice dripping from the trees and frozen pools clasping the blackened soil near the roots. My fingers felt like snapping off the bone when I opened and closed them. Across from the hospital was the bus stop made of mortared cinderblocks. When we got off the bus, a scrap of paper tumbled up the sidewalk and stuck on the wrought-iron gate of the hospital entrance.

We went to the hospital because Magda had come home crying with pain. She splashed vomit on the front step, and when she tried to rise, swooned and crashed against the screen door. Mom and I were in the kitchen. She was sewing a button on a shirt, and I was scraping the dirty moons under my fingernails. Mom jumped up right away and rushed out the door screaming in panic. Not knowing what the screaming was about, I thought something crazy had happened, like maybe some rabid dog had snuck into the kitchen or a giant rat poked its head out of a hole, two things of which I knew my mom was terrified. I dashed out behind her.

At first I thought Magda had gotten hit by a car. The crosswalk over by Walnut Street had no stop sign, and the street winds around a curve so sharp that cars boom down on you before you know it. But the way she was cramping and bundling her stomach, I thought it was food poisoning, like my aunt Letty, who came back from Mexico with amoebas. But Magda didn't look stiff and glassy-eyed like I'd seen dogs that had been hit by a car look, and she wasn't moaning in a way that showed amoebas had knotted her up. When I got close, I noticed a red carnation of blood blooming on the lap of her dress.

Mom had her suspicions. She pulled me over and told me to help drag Magda inside. Gossip had a way of spreading around the housing projects quicker than dry burning grass.

Mom's suspicions proved right. Magda was losing a baby. Mom figured it out by the stiff way Magda clutched her belly which you could see was swollen even under the loose dress. Mom had lost two babies herself; one was born dead; the other birthed too early to start life complete, and died in the hospital incubator after only a couple of hours of sucking air. Mom said you could have put her little baby girl inside a shoebox, she was so tiny.

We dragged Magda, muscle stiff and clumsy, across the cement floor to the bathroom. She was hooking her fingers into tiny crevices in the air and whenever she whined, a menthol chill the size of a maple leaf touched on my neck.

It took some pulling to drag her to the bathroom, but as soon as we stopped, Mom said to me, "Get out!," and grabbed my arm to shove me back through the door. I didn't know why we were in the bathroom, or what the hell exactly was the matter with Magda, so I sort of wrestled with Mom there at the door. I didn't really try too hard, and she was strong as a bear. She slammed the door against my hands.

I stood outside not knowing how long and not really thinking about anything. Then I opened the door. Magda had her coat off, and her head was leaning against the toilet. Right beside her, as if it had just spit out between her legs, was this tiny baby laying there like a slimy puppy with a big head and no hair and smeared in a dirty blue-purple jam. Its mouth was puckered shut, its teeny arms were raised and tight like a wrestler flexing victory, and its bitsy fingers spread out as if to grab a marble. Mom fumbled a little with the braid it was tied to and threw the baby in the toilet.

On the bus ride to the hospital, Mom cried and moaned about not following her instincts and asking questions. She should have pulled the *bruta*, my sister, weeks ago by the hair and demanded explanations. She was only thankful to the Lord that Dad wasn't home. She forced her voice through gritted teeth and warned me not to tell him.

Hearing Dad's name, Magda started whining and blubbering, and people on the bus turned around. The way the nosy bus driver eyed us in the rearview, I could tell he thought we were some crazies. I gave him a criminal stare, and showed all the people in the bus that we weren't a family to be messed with.

It was after we reached our stop in front of the hospital and began steering Magda toward the Emergency entrance that I noticed the cold. It was warmer in the Emergency Room, though. While Mom filled out the admission forms, I sat with Magda on the scratchy orange seats made of plastic and black tubing. Her hair was sweaty and plastered on her forehead, and she kept drawing up her legs, cradling herself small. She shuddered and moaned, and every time she did, a shovel blade churned earth inside my stomach. Once I made the mistake of touching her head, and she whimpered, loud.

The receptionist, a Mexican lady like us, kept sighing and shaking her head. Mom kept opening and closing her old lint-bally coat, then finally took it off. She had tried for months to get Dad to buy her a long beige coat with buttons big as fifty-cent pieces that she'd seen at Penney's. Dad mostly refused, raising his hand as if to visor his eyes against the sun. Sometimes he'd promise to buy her one at the end of the month, knowing that the bills would always manage to wedge in between her and the coat. One day she came home saying that she'd gone to the store and the coat wasn't there. The saleslady said they'd run out of stock. It didn't matter, Mom said. She'd gotten used to wearing her old linty coat and double sweaters. You could tell by the watery way her voice sounded, though, that she hated that coat. She just didn't want to give my dad the satisfaction of denying her something he knew she wanted.

She came out from behind the cubicle and creeped over to whisper in my ear. "That lady could make Santa Claus grumble," she said, pointing to where the receptionist was watching.

That was just like my mom, I thought, always making jokes about things people did to us. She'd tell it later to our neighbor Sophie, for sure, like it was the funniest story in the world. When she said this about the receptionist, I knew then that the lady's sighs were not out of sympathy, or embarrassment, or even curiosity; they were sighs of disapproval.

In the waiting room, there were two people with sick, droopy faces, and another with a broken finger or wrist. Sitting next to us was a man with a gash on his head. He was pressing a ball of baby diapers against his forehead. His wife told us that they'd been standing on a curb when one of those plumbing trucks cut around the corner, and a pipe sticking out of the back hit her husband smack on the forehead, knocking him out. She said she was terrified and couldn't find help. She thought at first that the guys in the truck didn't notice, but now that she remembers it, she did hear the engine winding down as if to stop, then pick up speed again. She said it was funny how she didn't remember this before, and how her memory came back to her at that very moment. Her husband, with his one eye peeking, gave her a look like, *Oh, please.*

She made me nervous, that lady, the way she kneaded her hands and fussed over her husband who got all steamed when he heard how those guys gassed the pedal after knocking him out. What made it worse was that he couldn't talk. Every time he widened his throat to say something, a tiny trickle of blood streamed down the lobe of his ear. He couldn't tilt back on the seats either, because of the angle of his wound. So he just sat there, shoulders straight and forehead pointing to the ceiling.

After a while, Mom grabbed my arm and said Magda needed to go pee. I helped walk her down the hall. We were so busy keeping her head from flopping over that we walked into the men's restroom. I knew right away by the stink, and no doors on the toilet stalls, and all the crappers sprinkled with gold drops.

Before we could pull Magda out though, she fainted, and Mom panicked and ordered me to get the receptionist. As I ran out, sliding on the tile floor, I noticed Magda's head lying near some black heel scuffs.

I ran over to the receptionist, who was sitting stiffly behind her desk. She must have heard Mom shout, but looked at me without a smidgen of sympathy.

"We gotta get a doctor," I said when I reached her desk. "My sister's fainted. She's right there on the floor, fainted."

"Is that the men's restroom you went into?" the receptionist asked.

"Yeah, but . . ."

The receptionist surveyed me up and down, her face a windless puddle of water. She picked up some papers on her desk and shuffled them carefully in order, then removed an ink pen and flat marble penholder and placed them inside her desk drawer. She jiggled out a key from her pocket and locked it. Looking at me, her lips pressed and eyebrows like black lightning bolts, I couldn't tell whether she was embarrassed or angry.

When I got back to the restroom, Magda was on the floor, her muscles slack as water inside a balloon. I thought she was dead. The receptionist, who didn't seem panicky at all, stood straight over her with her arms and legs set in triangles. "She'll be all right," she said. "She's just weak, that's all. Once we get her inside the doctor will fix her right up." She tried to say this cheerfully, but when she saw my mother's face, she put her frown back on.

Mom stuck her hands under Magda's shoulders and lifted. "Let's go, honey, let's go see the doctor." Her hands kept sliding out from under Magda's armpits, and she kept drooping back to the floor. "Manny, get over here and help me," she said. "We got to get her inside the clinic." She turned to the receptionist and said in the politest voice she knew if she could please get a wheelchair.

"Okay, I will, but I'm sorry you won't be able to see the doctor right now."

My mother started to stand up but didn't. If she had, Magda's head would have whacked on the floor.

"It's only that the doctor can't see her right away," the receptionist explained. She had her eyes fixed on the scuff marks on the floor, blinking, her lips firm. "If you just go back to the waiting room, as soon as he's free, I'll call him, okay?"

Before Mom could answer, the receptionist snapped her eyes from the floor and rushed out, saying something I couldn't hear.

I was trying to get a hold under Magda's

shoulders when the receptionist came back, slam-
ming a wheelchair against the hydraulic door,
making me jump from the sudden bang and hiss.

I guess the receptionist hadn't finished with
her lecture about the doctor, because as soon as
she came in she started in on how all the doctors
work nonstop ten hours a day, sometimes nights,
how the whole staff are so dedicated. She knew,
because she herself had typed up the duty rosters.
She blew some more smoke about how people like
us expect everything to be fed to them on silver
spoons. How we never take responsibility. She
said that's why we're so confused and screwed up.
Only she didn't say "confused" and "screwed up,"
but said "neurotic" and another medical word I
couldn't make out.

Mom's shoulders began twitching, and any
minute I thought she was going to jump up and
tear the lady's hair out. But she was too busy
grabbing Magda under the arms and trying to
prop the wheelchair, which kept slipping, against
the door handle.

I was going to get up and tell the lady myself
to leave, but just then Magda turned to me, and
said my name, "Manny," real low and weak.

Finally, we got her into the wheelchair. The

receptionist held the hydraulic door and watched, her eyes a mushy boredom. She wasn't preaching anymore. She didn't even look embarrassed about her slobbery speech. If anything, it was my mom who looked embarrassed. She was rattled, too, by what the lady had said. She wasn't surprised, though. Nothing surprised my mom. She *expected* people to treat her mean. Then a little anger sparked inside her. When she turned the chair to wheel Magda out, she said in a gruff voice for me, *not* the lady, to hold open the door.

In the waiting room we sat down near the guy clenching his bloody diapers. I couldn't see much under the compress, but he was a bald guy with bulby, alcoholic ears and a sunburned neck. His wife had come over when she heard the commotion. Her fat rolled in different directions when she walked with us down the hallway.

The lady stopped at the coffee machine and plopped in some coins. The spout squirted out a dark, rusty water. She planned to give it to her husband, but from under his mountain of diapers, he peered at her like she was an idiot for even thinking he could drink from a cup.

She asked Mom if she wanted the coffee. Mom

took the coffee, gulped a mouthful, and braced it on her lap.

"These people," the lady said, sitting down beside my mom. "I can't stand them, either. It's like they care more about the *gavachos* than they do about us." She shook her head and stared at the floor.

I was sitting behind my mom and the lady. I saw Mom's shoulders begin to jiggle. She was crying. The lady reached out and put her hand on Mom's lap. As she did, a tear from Mom's eye dropped on her arm, and quickly, the lady rubbed it off, as if it burned. Then she looked up at her husband peeking at her from behind his barricade of diapers. He flinched his head, signaling with gritted teeth. He wanted her to keep to her own business and get back to taking care of him.

When we got back from the hospital it was early, but already dark. Dad was asleep and Nardo nowhere to be found. Pedi was at Sophie's. I went to my room and nestled under the covers, feeling wound-up and anxious, cringing down in bed. I must have fallen asleep, because when I heard moaning, I sat up in an eyeblink, and there was a gray shaft of morning light under the door, and Nardo was beside me, asleep.

I heard Mom through the walls, talking to herself. I wasn't sure if she was saying something about Magda or reminding herself of the chores needing to be done. Flopping off my side of the blankets, I called to her, then knocked lightly on the wall to see if I could get her attention. Dad heard me, and began mumbling curses about the pesty annoyance of kids, but he didn't get up.

Beside me, Nardo was a dark clump on the bed. I whispered to him, but there was no answer. His face could barely be seen in the murky darkness. I wondered whether I should wake him, but just as I was about to touch his shoulder, he snatched at the blanket and tucked himself into a cocoon. I saw a shadow flicker under the door and slipped out of bed.

Magda had been tumbling in fever, strangling phlegm in her throat and making gruff, coughy barks. When I got to her room, the bedsheet was moist and the blanket mussed from all her twisting. Sweat had glued her eyelids shut, and spit leaked out of her mouth and pushed a wet dent on the pillow. Mom, her eyes worried to slits, was sitting on the bed beside her, wondering aloud whether to take her back to the hospital. Her fever was worse than the doctor had said it'd get.

When she heard me, she ordered me to stay by the door. She didn't want me tugging her brain with questions. So I stayed where I was, staring over Mom's back as she loaded up a towel from a bowl of water, squeezed it, and washed away a smear of milky wetness from Magda's nose.

"Are we going to take her to the hospital?" I asked, worrying my finger on my T-shirt.

Mom turned, and after settling her eyes on me for about a second she looked above my shoulder. I followed her eyes and there, through a slit in the hallway, I could see my dad lying, the blankets kicked to his feet and his arm dangling over the side of the bed. He'd fallen back asleep as soon as he shouted for Mom to shut up the noise. He looked like a huge baby, but with a mustache and graying hair.

"Go back to sleep," Mom said, her face soft, "quit worrying about your sister." She went back to dampening her with a towel.

I stayed where I was, my eyes locked on the ruffles of her blue nightgown. "Mom, I think you better get Dad's keys so we can take her to the hospital again," I said, twisting my finger more on my shirt.

Mom shrunk her eyes narrow. "You listen to me, Manuel," she said, "if you don't get back to bed . . ." She stopped there. This was the voice she often used on me, but I was getting too big now to bow to her threats. If I remained stubborn, she'd usually call on Dad to come threaten me. But Dad didn't know what had happened, and she didn't want him finding out.

"I think we ought to take her to the hospital," I said as a low whine flowed from Magda.

Mom laid Magda's head gently back on the pillow. When she turned to me, a wildness showed in her eyes, and her right cheek fluttered like a nerve had blown out on that side of her face. She took the moistened rag and threw it with a splat near my feet. "I told *you* to go back to sleep," she said icily.

Then, suddenly, before I could say anything, or even lift my eyes from the wet rag, she rose, and with her hand cupped like a spoon, smacked me hard on the ear. I just stood there, bracing, but the blow was like a spike inside my ear, and I stumbled, my head butting against the side of the door. I collapsed on one knee and stayed there, gazing at the floor. When Mom spoke again, I lifted my face. I wasn't angry or afraid but could only plead at her with my eyes.

"Now, go back to sleep!" she said, her voice breaking.

I refused to budge. I kept holding my ear like it was an abscessed tooth. "You just don't want him to be mad at you," I said, with crevices in my voice.

Looking around like there was no place for her to hide her eyes, Mom shrieked, "We don't have any money!" Then, her face reddening with panic, she covered her mouth, afraid that any more yelling might wake up Dad.

Then, maybe to keep me from saying anything more, she struck me again, this time with mean, chopping strokes. Zigzags of lightning connected the seconds as she cut down smack after smack on my neck and on my shoulder. The air had a sharp, splintery edge. I arched my back, cowering, but I didn't want to raise my arm to cover myself, thinking she'd stop hitting me sooner if I didn't do anything.

When I finally looked up, Mom backed away, her eyes circles of panic and her long liquid hair drooping across her face. She pushed back some strands of hair and stood there, her nose flaring and her cheeks watery with tears. "*Mijo,* please, do what I say," she pleaded, sucking back a ribbon of saliva. Then her voice became tender, and she began to cajole me, saying, "Please, I *can't* wake him. He'll blame it on you for not watching over her. He'll say it's your fault. Come on, honey, go back to bed, I'll fix Magda up. Don't worry." Her last words wound to a slur, and a glassy trickle weeped over her chin.

I leaned against the wall, my arm dead to the coldness. "How's he gonna blame me?" I asked, in a voice that sounded like a girl's. "Who's he got to blame other than hisself?"

An aching, heavy gravity pulled down on my stomach when Mom looked at me, her face twisted with hurt over what I'd said. She hurt, I knew, because she didn't want to admit it to herself, afraid that she too was to blame. But just then, Dad sat up in bed with a jerking snort, his body creaking the bed springs. He was moaning from pain. From years of cranking tools and lifting sacks, the heels of his palms were anvils of yellow callus, and his back had slipped a disc. He couldn't move in the easy way he once did. Every time he rose from a couch or bed, he'd groan.

Mom turned to me with a stiff stare. I thought she'd stay frozen that way forever, when suddenly her eyes lifted over my shoulder. There, suddenly, in the doorway, was Dad. He put his hand on my shoulder, peering into the room. Even with his half-painful, half-sleepy eyes he figured out everything in a flash.

"Put her in water," he said to my mom in Spanish.

"But . . ."

"Put her in water," he said again, brusquely this time, then walked away wobbly and absent-minded.

I thought he was going back to bed, but then I saw a light blink on at the end of the hallway and heard water drumming into the bathtub. He came back pushing his way past me, and without a word grabbed Magda from the bed and with a mighty groan lifted her up.

Like an ant carrying a giant statue of bread, Dad carried Magda out of the room. I slid up beside him, bracing his arms. I knew his back was hurting. In the bathroom, Dad put Magda, night-gown and all, inside the tub and bobbed her steady. She floated a little, her gown blossoming in the water like a boat sail, and after a long while her eyes blinked open. She looked up at us staring down at her, and then, with a surprise that showed the fever had died, she looked at Dad, amazed. I don't know if it was because of the pain in his back, or the pain of seeing Magda sick, or both, but his face was trembling and red, as if blown by a hot, blurry wind.

■9■

Dying of Love

To Mom's surprise, Dad actually found a job doing office work for the Awoni Building Company. To everyone's surprise, Nardo got a job delivering medicine for Giddens's Pharmacy. I helped him with his route on Saturdays, when the weather was either snips of cold snagging fishhooks through your clothes, or just plain icy, with steam flowing from every breath. Nardo would keep the engine running while I bolted for the cash, or Medi-Cal card, whichever arrangement those old retired geezers had with the pharmacy. Afterward, we'd go to lunch in Chinatown and order hot plates of chow mein noodles and sweet-and-sour pork.

That Saturday I roused myself from bed, put on my red hunter's jacket and right away walked out into the thin ghosts of fog. I heard the kitchen faucet hissing, and saw Mom through the kitchen window squeezing a mop in the sink, humming as she shook out dirt from the strands. She was wearing her flower print dress, the one with the flowers faded, and rumpled like she'd crushed it in her hands before putting it on.

She always did chores before the sun blinked on the horizon, when she could think clear without a lot of kids yelling, or Sanchez, our neighbor with the blue Virgin tattooed across his back, gunning his car engine.

She began slapping the mop wildly on the floor, shuffling around in my dad's old hightop boots, the ones with the buckles torn out and tongues wagging. Most of the time she mopped the floor barefoot, since her feet had enough calluses to step on my dad's cigarette butts without making her wince, but that day it was too cold.

I heard more water moaning through the pipes, then a drumming in the bathtub. Dad was taking a bath and singing. For as long as I remember, especially when in a good mood, he sang this Mexican ballad that I never could figure out the words to. He'd repeat this one line over and over, *"Quiero morir de amor,"* or *"Quiero vivir con amor." I want to die of love;* or, *I want to live with love.* One or the other, I wasn't sure. Both phrases in Spanish sounded so alike.

When I neared the pharmacy, the sun was knifing a big blue hand through the ghosts of fog, sweeping them away like cobwebs. The maple trees on that street were dreary and weeping moisture, their stripped bark dusted with a glassy talcum of mist. But that, too, was melting. And when the wind came, little sneezes of drizzle sprayed on my face.

Nardo, who'd taken off earlier, should have been waiting outside, since he didn't want Mr. Giddens to find out I was working with him. I doubted if he'd get fired, though, since Nardo with my help was the fastest deliverer that old boss man had.

I waited outside, trying to keep my teeth from chattering. Finally, against the nagging in my head, I stepped inside.

Mr. Giddens was behind the counter, pouring pills with a plastic shovel into a jar. He had parched hands and a face hacked as if by baseball cleats. I acted casual over by the Get Well cards, pretending to read them and then jamming them back into the slots.

From the corner of my eye, I saw Mr. Giddens sizing me up. He put down what he was doing and came over. He had a mustache of sweat and tiny diamond necklaces under his eyes. Figuring he'd lose more money from thievery than gas bills, he kept the store steaming hot, so that everybody who came in would have to take off their coats and hang them on a tree rack by the door. I didn't take off my coat, and that's why Mr. Giddens noticed me.

Steering his finger toward the storage room in the back, he said, "You and Bernard better get your butts cracking, all the other boys are gone."

"Yes sir, Mr. Giddens," I said, hurrying down the aisle. "We'll get going right away. . . . I mean, I'll tell my brother to get going."

"Don't think I don't know about you two working together," he shouted after me, wiping his face with a handkerchief. "I wasn't born yesterday."

Nardo was busy sorting out prescriptions in a cardboard box. Other guys hoarded routes that gave tips, or had addresses near their homes, so they could knock off for lunch. Nardo didn't need to, since most of the guys lived across town, and our side of town didn't give any tips.

Acting annoyed when I came in, Nardo nodded and kept counting the bags of prescriptions. In the storage room there were packing crates full of empty soda bottles. I put my finger into the hole of a Dr Pepper. "You ready?"

"Yeah, let's get going."

"We still going to Chinatown?"

"Yeah, we're still going to Chinatown!" he said, still annoyed. "I think we should finish all the deliveries before we eat, though, don't you?"

"If you say so."

"Yeah, I say so," he said. "Hey, and what's the deal coming in through the store?" He put the box down on a chair and shook his coat before putting it on. "What did the old fart say, anyway?"

"I think he knows we're working together."

"For crying out loud—I knew he'd find out," he said, pushing his fingers through his hair. "Well, if we don't admit it, I think it'll be all right."

To keep up the pretending, I went back in through the store with the idea of going around to the alley, where Nardo would pick me up.

That's when I saw Dorothy, Mr. Giddens's daughter, although I didn't know her name or who she was at the time. She was standing over by the Get Well cards where I'd stood, raising her arms in the air and talking excitedly to Mr. Giddens. She kept turning heatedly away from him, as if to puzzle over some hot question, then she'd whirl around and say stuff like, "You're kidding!" or "That's hard to believe!"

When she saw me, she smiled, like she recognized me, then turned back around to Mr. Giddens who looked at me like suddenly an idea had popped into his head.

"Oh, Manuel! Could you come over here a minute," he said, bending his arm around in a little corral. "I want to introduce you to my daughter."

He kept circling his hand for me to come over, but I couldn't get my shoes to budge. Something was screwed on wrong. Mr. Giddens inviting me over to introduce me to his daughter wasn't natural. He hardly ever talked to Nardo, and the only time he'd ever even talked to me was on that day, and then only to yell at me.

"Dorothy, this is one of my delivery boys, Manuel, uh, Hernandez—or is it Herrera?"

"Hernandez."

"Oh yeah," he said, tossing his hand flightily in the air. "I get Bernard confused as well." He smiled and looped his arm around me.

Dorothy wore a beige skirt and a thinly woven sweater with cord designs. Her hair was clipped in high bangs on her forehead. Close up, her shoulders and hair smelled like a peach orchard with the wind coming through it, and there was a sort of mushy softness to her face, like she'd carefully massaged oils and special creams into it. Her nose was small, with the most delicious angles, and she had a moony way of looking at me that got me all buttery inside.

"Hi, Dorothy!" I said, anxious to meet her, yet stiffening a little against Mr. Giddens's push.

"Hi," she said, smiling.

She wanted to talk more with her father, but he didn't want to. He clamped both his hands on my shoulders.

"You know, Dorothy," he said, "one day Manuel is going to be my best deliverer. Right now I have him training with his brother Bernard. He's too young to have a license, but as soon as he gets one, he's going to have a job right here."

"But Dad! What about the cards?" she said, taking a big step forward.

"Oh, the cards! Is that all you want? Well, go ahead, take as many as you like." He waved his hand carelessly along the aisle. "If you want more, there's boxes of them in the back. Here, I'll get Manuel to help you."

"I already have the ones I want," Dorothy said, tapping the stack of cards she had in her hand against her other wrist.

"Oh, well, I'll tell you what. How many do you have there?"

Dorothy tilted her head slightly, and one of her eyes shrunk with suspicion. "Fifteen?" she said.

"Fifteen, huh. I'll tell you what. Get one more. Make it an even sixteen. I'm sure Manuel here would like to go. What do you say? Would you like to come to Dorothy's party? Lots of food and punch?"

He said this enthusiastically, wiping his face with a handkerchief, but while he did, Dorothy was tightening her shoulders and her smile collapsed a little. "Dad!!" she said, stressing her voice.

"No—no—I'm serious about this, now. I think Manuel would like to come. Wouldn't you, Manuel? Sure—sure, you'd like to come."

"Daad!!!" Dorothy said again, and this time her smile vanished. She struggled to hold her hands to her sides. I could see the bones on her chest stretching from the muscle, like little wing-blades about to take flight.

"Do you know what, dear?" Mr. Giddens said, his eyes sparkling. "Now that I think of it. Maybe some of the *other* delivery boys would like to come to your party. Maybe I'll ask *them*."

"They're too old!" Dorothy exclaimed. "You're

166

going to spoil it, Dad. You're going to mess it all up like you always do!" Her face was glowing with defiance.

"Well, maybe you're right, honey," Mr. Giddens said, putting his hand on his waist and eyeing Dorothy as if figuring out a complicated math problem. "Maybe just Manuel, then—huh, sweetheart?"

An idea snapped inside Dorothy's head. She turned hopefully to me. "Maybe he doesn't *want* to come, Dad?"

"Sure he wants to come! Don't you Manuel?" Mr. Giddens said, egging me on.

"Well," I said. I didn't know what to say, really; didn't know what was going on. Whatever was going on, though, I knew words wouldn't help.

"But he won't *know* anybody," Dorothy pleaded.

"That's what you'll be there for, honey," Mr. Giddens said with assurance, "to introduce him around, make him feel welcome. I'm positive he'll have a good time."

"Okay . . . okay. I give up!" Dorothy said, gritting her teeth and dropping her arms, exasperated. She handed me an invitation card. "Here, you're invited," she said halfheartedly.

167

Despite being angry, Dorothy had a smooth, floating look about her as she walked quickly away, like she was being lifted by the applause in a theater full of people. I remembered then a vase I once saw at the Kern Museum. It belonged to some rich people who first settled our town, and it was beautiful. Not the vase, actually, but everything inside and around the vase. The tinted petals of the roses, the white flowers, tiny as gnats, and the deep, glowing nut-color of the mahogany table. Everything seemed so perfect. And the vase held it all together. I remembered thinking if somebody were to come in at that exact moment and lift that vase off the table, the whole room and everything in it would collapse.

Before walking out of the door, Dorothy turned and smiled. It was a smile that would tumble around inside my brain for days. I wanted to believe that it meant that somehow she'd changed her mind about me, and that I'd be welcome at her party, but deep down I knew it didn't. In any case I didn't care, and only later, when I realized that I *should* have cared, did it really hurt.

Just then I felt someone's eyes on the back of my neck. It was Nardo near the storage door staring at me. He was smiling, too, but a mocking smile, like he sure didn't envy my predicament.

We went straight home after work, not stopping in Chinatown. Nardo was anxious to tell everybody in the world about Dorothy. He took off his coat and flung it into the living room, missing by a breath the shelf where Mom displayed her miniature animals. He rushed over to Magda, who was eating cornmeal mush at the yellow Formica table, and said, "Hey, do you know what? Manny's got the hots for Mr. Giddens's daughter!"

"Mr. Giddens has a daughter?"

"Yeah, and pretty, too. At least I think she's pretty, underneath all that snobby makeup. But you shoulda seen Manny." He pointed at me. "He got all mushy and red over her. Boy, was it a sad sight. I thought his jaw was going to drop off."

"My jaw wasn't doing nothing," I said sullenly.

"Hey, what can I say?" He arched his eyebrows and sprouted ten, innocent fingers. "If Mr. Giddens notices, anybody can."

"Nobody notices nothing," I said, sinking into a chair.

"*Nobody notices nothing,*" Nardo mimicked.

169

He shook me teasingly on the shoulder. "You should of heard what he said when you went out through the front door. Aw, you don't want to know about that?" He slapped me on the shoulder.

I was dying to know, but I wasn't about to admit it to him. If I even hinted that I was interested, he wouldn't tell me for as long as he could torture me by not telling. I could feel his and Magda's superior eyes on me, grins stretching back to their ears. When I looked up, they shut down their smiles and exchanged nods.

"Is there any more cornmeal?" Nardo asked, his voice a deep echo inside the open refrigerator.

"No, I just made this for me," Magda said, innocently pinching cornmeal from her lip. "Mom said to wait till she got back. She's gonna buy Fig Newtons to eat until she fixes dinner."

"Fig Newtons, huh?" Nardo said, casual as could be. He acted like nothing was going on, but I could tell he knew he had me hooked. He closed the door and stared at the ceiling, his eyes icing over.

"Don't you know what's going on, stupid!?" he burst out suddenly. "Mr. Giddens and his wife are going to be out of town. He just wants you to spy on his daughter's party while he's away."

Shaking her head, Magda lurched forward. She had food in her mouth and had to swallow before talking. "You mean she didn't invite him?" she asked, choking.

"No."

"Yeah, she did!"

"Boy, are you going to be out of place there!" Magda said, shaking her head.

"He don't listen. He thinks he's really been invited."

"She gave me an invitation," I said, hotly.

"Yeah, an invitation with nothing written on it."

"They'll probably make him wash dishes," Magda put in.

"No, they'll tell him to feed the dog."

Magda pushed her cornmeal away, afraid she'd tip it over while she laughed, but spilled some anyway.

"Aw, you guys could kiss lemons for all I care," I said, pushing back my chair.

"Yeah, I know what *you* wanna kiss," Nardo howled.

"Is that true?" Magda asked, glassy-eyed with laughter, but fighting to be serious. "Do you really *like* that white bitch?"

"She's not a bitch!" I said, even hotter.

"So, you do! You do like her!" she exclaimed. She leaned back on her chair, beaming, as if remembering something savory. "Boy, I thought you had better sense than to fall for some white girl."

"You guys ain't funny—you know that? You ain't funny!"

"Oh, I wasn't trying to be funny. It was Nardo who was trying to be funny," Magda said, jerking her thumb at him. "I was trying to figure out why Chicano guys are always falling for white girls—that's all."

That's when, my skin blazing, I stomped out the door, knowing that their teasing wasn't going to let up. I began rushing across the yard when suddenly I stopped, remembering that it was best not to go more than a sprinter's distance from the house, since the Garcia brothers roamed the projects like a pack of ferocious dogs. I lingered over my mom's pruned rosebushes, fingering the ashy thorns on the stems. I pricked my finger and out popped a small globe of blood. It tasted like copper.

Inside the kitchen, I could hear them laughing in lightning spurts, gorging on their own stupid wisecracks. Magda kept calming herself, then bursting out again in wild giggles. Finally, she said something about what a poor baby I was and scolded Nardo for being so mean. Then Nardo said something nasty that started her laughing all over again.

Maybe they were right, though. Maybe this was all a big joke to Mr. Giddens. All I knew was that for days after I couldn't pluck Dorothy's smile out of my mind. I was locked in long mental tortures of remembering her every move, her defiant eyes when arguing with Mr. Giddens, the fast fall of her blond hair when she crooked her neck, her bored fingers fluttering along the shelves when she pretended not to be listening. I even found myself thinking for hours over the designs of wind that wove behind her when she walked out of the store.

A flash of shame bloomed in my face, because when I focused my eyes, there, suddenly, in front of me, was Magda. "Boy, you really *are* hurting," she said, shaking her head. "You're going to get in trouble, you know that? If I was you I wouldn't go to that party," she warned.

"Well, you're not me. Besides, look who's talking about white people."

Magda just stared at me like she didn't believe what I'd said. She went back inside, listlessly waving her hand in the air. "Just don't get burned, that's all I gotta say. Don't get burned."

Once she had closed the door behind her, Nardo right away began laughing again, but she didn't join in.

For days I suffered the joy and terror of wanting to go to Dorothy's party, and knowing that it would be a big mistake. It was like a loose tooth you keep wiggling with your tongue, slow and deliberate, teasing the pain. The pain, however, wasn't in my mouth, but inside my chest. I fought against it. I'd stare hard into the mirror and order myself over and over to be strong . . . be a man! But then a cold fluttering would begin in the pit of my chest and before I could stop it, it'd spurt up a misty burning in my throat and eyes. My mind was speeding anxiously, gobbling up whole chunks of anticipation. At first, time seemed slow and heavy, but then faster and lighter—lighter until the day of the party, when the waiting became like no weight at all. Even so, I began to panic when Nardo pulled our Plymouth up in front of Mr. Giddens's house.

It was a cold night, but I was soaked in dread and could barely breathe. I was trying to be casual, so that Nardo wouldn't catch on and tease me, but he knew something was up and snatched me by the arm. "Hey, don't stick your foot in shit in there. You know what I mean?"

"No."

"It might stink."

"Oh."

When I opened the car door, the cold gushed in. The car had no heater, so when I spoke, clouds puffed from my mouth.

"Hey, Nardo," I said, turning back, "what do you think I should do?"

Nardo revved the engine lightly. It turned off if you didn't gas the pedal. "I don't know," he said, thinking. "Maybe you should try to have fun." He let the engine rumble. "What's wrong with that?"

"Nothing."

"Well, hey, don't worry. They're just a bunch of stuck-up *gavachos*." He smiled, pinched his lips shut and crunched the car into reverse. The car wound backward down the street and veered before going forward.

I walked toward the house, my breath fogging the air, my shoes cracking lines of geometry on the frozen lawn. The grasping night air, the far-off streetlights flashing, and the windows of the other houses on the block closing like eyelids too tired to stay awake, left me stiff with dread. Then a chill wind prowled under my jacket-wing and climbed to my ribs, making my lips burr. I zippered the jacket up and went up the porch steps.

A friend of Dorothy's answered the door. He was a husky, autumn-leaf-haired guy with a face spattered with freckles. He stood by the door, I suppose to welcome people as they came. I figured he was Dorothy's boyfriend, because he stood beside her, his brilliant white kernels of teeth blaring.

Dorothy had on a pleated gray skirt and white blouse ironed even under her arms and on the tips of her collar. Her hair, flared back in curls, was clasped by a black barrette with tiny diamonds on it, and she was wearing earrings. She had a drowsiness to her eyes, but when she smiled, her whole face gladdened like she was admiring a cute baby.

"How are you *doing*, Manuel?" she said, like these were the first words she'd used all day.

"I'm doing real good, thank you," I said, surprised that words even came from my mouth.

"Well, come inside, it's cold out there," she said, fussily.

I put on this big, smeary smile and urged my legs forward. My lungs felt big as balloons. There was a song by the Rolling Stones on the record player. I was nervous, but once I put my hand on the back of my neck, trying to look casual, I felt better.

Even in the darkness, I sensed the eyes of Dorothy's friends wondering who I was. Silent messages passed down the line of girls sitting on the long leather couch. The guys, standing by the large frosted windows, were staring hard at me. They were about my age or a little older, dressed in ironed slacks, wool sweaters and blazers.

One guy left a window and offered a hand to a girl sitting on one of the couches. She refused with a bored shrug, signaling the side of her face toward me. The guy nodded, and walked into the brightly-lit kitchen.

Then a girl with hair fluffed airy and wispy like cotton candy came over. She was tiny waisted, her face spotted with brown freckles. "Hi," she said, eyeing me up and down. "I'm Gloria."

"I'm Manuel. I work at Dorothy's father's store." I sort of stumbled with the words "Dorothy's father's store," but she nodded her head like she understood.

"Oh, I know," said the girl. "I know—she told me all about it."

Dorothy was not far away. She was talking in whispers to the red-haired guy, who was nodding his head up and down. Then she drifted around the room, speaking into people's ears and looking up at me. I snuck glances at her as she moved around the room, knowing that something about me was being exchanged, yet at the same time not caring. I remembered her smile at the store, and for some strange reason its effect on me was like a powerful light splashing around inside me, chasing away the shadows.

The turntable spun a slow song and the lights dimmed. Everybody began to dance, melting into a warm darkness of bodies. I was relieved, for a moment, because I felt that maybe they'd forgotten about me. I was almost sure of it when Gloria clasped my arm and led me to the middle of the dance floor. She linked her hands in mine, and a guy I didn't know cheerfully saluted us from across the room with a Dixie cup. We breathed on each other, Gloria breathing normal and me almost not at all, although I could smell the powder of her shoulders and perfume behind her ears.

As we danced, I saw Dorothy with the red-haired guy not far from us, her hand pressed against his chest. He had a drink of rum in one hand, and in the other, a cigarette, which he casually puffed on, but removed when he leaned over to whisper into Dorothy's ear. He said something, and dropped his eyes down the neck of her blouse.

Dorothy looked cool and fresh, as if carved from night air. The way her shoulders lifted, the way her heels didn't sway when she danced, the way the hem of her skirt fluttered, as if the air itself was swishing out of her way, touched my skin with a strange warmth, like I was being deliciously licked all over by tiny tongues of flame. I envied Red-Hair.

But this dreamy stumbling over Dorothy caused me to hug Gloria a bit too close, and not fit into her dancing rhythm. My leg accidentally slid between her legs. She got angry right away. "Hey, what's going on here? What do you think you're doing?"

I stepped back, startled, the brittle feeling of my dream collapsing, but I didn't say anything. Later, when I thought about it, after I ran it over

179

and over in my mind, I realized that that was a mistake. I should have said I was sorry right away. I should have kept my voice close. By stepping back, everybody's eyes focused on us. When I told Nardo later what had happened, he said that it wouldn't have mattered what I did.

The lights blinked on, and the guy playing the records abruptly took the needle off the grooves. People groaned.

Although he looked like he didn't totally know what was going on, Red-Hair grabbed my arm and pulled me away—not hard or jerking, but firm, as if ushering me out of a place I wasn't supposed to be.

"I told you what he's up to," I heard Dorothy say with coughy dryness.

Before I could half free my arm to say something, I noticed her from the corner of my eye twirl around and walk swiftly into the kitchen, her skirt flapping.

Still a bit puzzled but determined that it was his show now, Red-Hair let my arm go. There was a group of about four older guys in front of me, blocking my way to the door. They weren't big guys, nor did they look particularly mean, but there were four, and I didn't know them. For a short, dissolving second, I thought of shouldering my way through them and hurrying for the door, but they had these tense, questioning looks, and I was beginning to feel needles on my skin.

Instead of bumping into them, I took a step toward a sliding glass door on my right, and slid it open enough to squeeze out.

It led to a backyard, which like the house, was enormous. There were trees and bushes everywhere, and the grass went on for about a half a block and glowed with an icy sheen. I looked up, and the sky had a sort of bright raspiness to it, like dark water becoming slack after boiling. The air was chilly, but my chest hurt not from the cold, but from a feeling of everything being empty, as if inside my lungs there were only echoes.

I began to walk anxiously back and forth along the side of the house, seaching for an opening. The yard was surrounded by a high cedar fence, brown and slivering where some of the wood had curled with age. If I climbed it, I'd get splinters. I passed the glass door, and from the light of the outside lamp I saw the reflection of a ridiculous boy, a clumsy boy. It was me, looking at myself, except that it wasn't me, but someone ghostly and strange.

Then a shadow came across my reflection. Thinking for a second that it was Dorothy, my heart gulped.

"What are you doing out here, pal?" Red-Hair said, his voice like an electrical current traveling underwater. He was standing near me, his head glowing in the bright light that just then darkened with the heads of more guys. "I hear crazy things about you, buddy. Crazy things."

Red-Hair was rolling a piece of gum between his teeth and looking back at his friends as they began to fan out around the side of the house as though inspecting the grass and flowerbeds for snails. He leaned up close to me, almost touching my shoulder, then looked off to the far end of the yard. The outside lamp shone hard on half his face, and I could see the muscles of his jaw pulsing.

"You know, guys like you are weird ducks," he said, in a loud, but lazy voice. "You just hang around, quacking and flapping your little paddle feet. Do you know what I mean?"

I felt like a piece of cold steel was caught in my throat.

Noticing that I wasn't saying anything, Red-Hair went on, moving his chin in little jerks.

"Well, let me just say this, pal. I don't care if you are supposed to be a guest. This is not your party, and I don't like you coming around here bothering Dorothy." The last part he said with a hard pop of his gum as he ground his teeth into it.

I wanted to tell him that it was all a mistake, that Mr. Giddens made me come, and that I wasn't dying of love anymore, but I knew my brain was just searching for excuses.

Whether Red-Hair sensed what I was thinking, or whether he just thought he'd said enough, he smiled and shook his head at his friends. He put his thick palm on my shoulder, and in an almost friendly way, conked me a couple of times on the head with the large knuckle of his hand. Then, still chewing his gum hard, he turned toward the sliding glass door.

There, standing by the open curtain, was Dorothy. She was delicately biting a cuticle and looking worriedly at us, a crowd of curious girl-friends behind her.

Cocking his head back, Red-Hair walked toward her. He didn't say anything, but nodded and raised both his hands, first at me, than at her, as if to say, *Was this enough?*

■10■

A Test of Courage

The whole disaster with Dorothy Giddens made me realize that I wasn't anywhere close to being smooth with girls. Not so much because I was ugly, although I was *kind* of ugly, or that I was a pest, although my sister Magda would argue different. It was because I was too chicken to ever say anything to a girl— chicken with the sourest yellow. Just thinking about telling a girl I liked her clamped the muscles on my chest and made my lungs pull hard to catch a breath.

Not that girls spit on my shadow or anything, but I would never be sweet enough to threaten cavities even to a girl like Imelda Rodriguez, who wore bottle glasses and had teeth going every which way. Imelda wore clodhopper shoes and dragged a heavy shadow. I imagined her love would be a terrible howl of loneliness. But I would have adored her forever if, just once, she'd have tapped me with a shy finger of love.

I told my friend Frankie about this. He lived

near the irrigation canal at the far end of our projects, banked with scraggly oak trees and tall, speary grasses. Polliwogs wiggled away from approaching shadows and striped-green garter snakes twined inside the leafy beds of dead stumps. It was a fun place to play, sometimes.

Frankie said he knew what I meant, but that girls nowadays were impossible to talk to, although he knew where I could get to know this girl real good, if I wanted, and easy. I gulped like I'd just swallowed a delicious worm and said, "Really?"

"Yeah, really. Tomorrow—I'll show you."

A red blush of sky was giving in to silver patches of moonlight when Frankie and I set out for Mondo's house in the Callaway Projects. There, we found some guys hanging around a backyard. One was Mondo, another was his half-brother, Eddie. A guy called Gody whose real name was Guillermo was also there. And there were two girls named Rita and Patty inside the house.

Somebody had been using the yard to fix cars; it didn't have a lick of grass on it, only packed-in dirt stained with oil. Bald tires lay scattered around, and a chinaberry tree near the fence had a pulley chain hanging from a branch. The greasy chinaberries crudded my tennis shoes.

Frankie said if I wanted to sit down I could stand up a tire and crunch it down with my butt. I looked at the streaks of black grime on the rump of one of the tires and decided to stay standing.

Along the backyard was an alley with a gapped-out wooden fence. Broken boards dangled from rusted nails. Frankie told me that Eddie, Mondo's half-brother, cracked the planks with his foot when he drank too much and got angry about his mom dying of cancer. He warned me not to mention anything about mothers to Eddie. "When he starts going on about how you don't know shit, just shut your mouth, okay?"

Rita and Patty were inside Mondo's room, which you could get into from the back porch. I wanted to join the gang because Frankie promised that I could kiss and make out with one of the girls when I passed the initiation. I was anxious about it, and curious about how the girls looked.

That's when Patty came out. She had beer-color eyes and black hair plowed down the middle, flowing down almost to her hips. I remembered seeing her at school, her hair in the sun glowing like a fiery blue jelly. She wore cowboy boots and high black socks that led up to a miniskirt so tight against her hips that she had to turn her legs a little sideways to walk.

Patty smiled daisies at Frankie and play-tugged on Gody's sleeve, but her best eyes she saved for Mondo, making flirty winks and talking with a throaty voice. He craned his neck back, rubbed his wrist and smiled with slit eyes. Me, she ignored, and went back into the house.

She was supposed to be Mondo's girlfriend, but Frankie didn't know for sure. He searched the clouds whenever I asked about her. That didn't stop him from making up stories when I got cold about joining the gang. He also said Rita wasn't as pretty as Patty, but said she'd let anybody kiss her, and that thought clawed at my throat, as did the way he referred to the girls as *pollitas,* which in Spanish meant "little chicks." The word sent a current of excitement rushing through my chest.

With the brim of his *pachuco* hat turned down, Mondo went around collecting dues. The plan was to buy a car. They figured he could drive, him being seventeen and having a beginner's license. His aunt signed the papers at the DMV because he promised he'd take her to buy groceries when he bought the car. She wasn't so smart.

In any case, Mondo didn't want a bunch of guys hogging up the seats, so they figured a few *vatos firmes*, firm guys, would do the trick.

"Hey, *ése*, are you a *vato firme*?" he said holding out the hat. His eyes stared at me from far away.

"Yeah, *ése*." I dug into my pocket and took out all my change, about eighteen cents, and dropped it in the hat.

"Did you give him the lowdown?" he asked Frankie.

"Yeah, I told him."

The lowdown was that I had to pass the Test of Courage to become a member of the Callaway Projects gang. I'd also get to make out with Rita, which, as I found out later, was a rule made up while trying to decide if girls were even going to be in the gang. Rita suggested it, although she added that she wouldn't let anybody actually lie down with her. She didn't mind making it seem close, though.

It was one of those evenings when the moon comes out early and looks scarred with a dark rash. Mondo passed around some Lucky Strike cigarettes, shoving them out like tubes and watching to see if we were thankful or greedy.

"So," he said, "Frankie says you been to Juvy."

"No—I never been to Juvy," I said. I was embarrassed about having to admit it. Frankie must have told him I'd been in Juvenile Hall to impress him.

"Well, I been to Juvy," Mondo said, "once." He nodded slowly, getting everybody's attention and lit his cigarette. He handed me the match, and when he did, I caught a glimpse of a tattoo in the shape of a C on the fleshy bridge between his thumb and forefinger. "Me and some guys from Holloway Projects got caught stealing this car. We didn't mean nothing by it. We was jus' going to cruise around and drink beer, go check out the *rucas* on Belmont Avenue. We used to do it all the time, you know. We'd take the car and dump it over by Chinatown. The owner'd get it back the next day, sometimes with more gas in the tank than when we got it."

He winked over at Frankie, his cigarette pinched between his fingers, then took a giant drag, letting the smoke pour out between his lips in a tight blue vapor. "You ever stole a car?" he asked, choking a little.

"No, sorry," I said, regretting again my mousy admission.

189

"Never?" Mondo asked, in mock surprise. He turned sideways and raised an eyebrow at the guys. I thought he was going to make fun of me, but then he said, "Ahh, don't worry about it. It ain't no big deal, really, it ain't no big deal." He spit out a speck of tobacco, then walked over to the fence and flipped his cigarette into the alley. It hit a puddle somewhere and made a sizzle. "Besides, we ain't stealing any more cars. Ain't that right, Frankie?"

Frankie was searching for matches. He found a book and began lighting everybody's cigarettes, all except Eddie's, who had hooked his behind his ear. I hadn't smoked my own cigarette either and couldn't remember what I did with the match Mondo handed me.

"*Chale*, those days are gone," Frankie said, arching his shoulders.

"*Simón ése*, those days are gone," Mondo agreed. He puffed his cigarette again, then crooked his fingers in the shape of a claw and circled them around. "We're going to buy a car, *ése*— all of us, except, maybe . . . you." He shook his fingers out, sweeping them over everybody, then curled them in again, leaving only his thumb out, the one with the tattoo. He pointed it at me. "It depends on whether you pass the test. Right, Frankie?"

"I tell you," Frankie said, with exaggerated toughness, "he's Bernardo's brother. He'll prob'ly kick all our asses."

"Not mine. He won't kick my ass!" Eddie said, stepping out of the dark of the alley. He'd been listening near the fence. There was threat in his voice, and his face was gluey from drinking Night Train. He had long hair, almost as straight as mine, moss thin and blond, and a pale, bedsheet-color face. His eyes were nickel blue, like light flitting off the shank of a sharpened knife.

"Calm down, Eddie," Frankie said. "I was *only* kidding."

Eddie smiled, like he got one over on Frankie, then lit his cigarette.

When Frankie had first told me about the initiation, I pumped my fists in the air with showy bravery. The initiation was to test a guy's courage. You could either sissy out, or have Mondo think you brave enough to stand the punishment.

Actually, it wasn't the pain of getting socked and kicked that bothered me, but more the pain of feeling afraid. When chicken feathers choke in your veins, being afraid could be a real knife in the ribs. Then any disgrace is possible. I worried that I'd start begging, maybe even drop to the ground, paralyzed with fear, like in the war movies when the bombs drop, shocking the dirt.

When Mondo announced the beginning of the initiation, a rash of alarm broke over my skin. Patty and Rita came out from the back porch, Patty still wearing her tight skirt, and Rita a rusty leather jacket about three sizes too big. She was giggling one of those long streamer giggles, and looking at her, I felt mushy around my shoulders. She had on those wrinkly short pants that flared like trombones. There was a crease between her legs, like somebody had lightly tapped a finger there.

As they walked slowly down the concrete steps, past the blistered paint on the screen door, the late moonlight shadows stretched lazily across the greasy yard.

Mondo invited the girls to watch. But only if they weren't squeamish, he said, winking at me. Then, without a word of warning or even a nod signaling a beginning, Mondo and Eddie began circling around me. Frankie and Gody snuck glances at each other, their faces rubbery, like they'd been slapped. I knew they weren't the serious ones.

Suddenly Eddie dropped to the ground, and before I could lift my leg, he hooked his left ankle behind my heel and shoved at my knee with his right foot. My knee hinge locked and I fell backward on my butt. I whirled around quickly, almost flailing to stand up, but before I did, Mondo clamped his hands on my head and forced me down.

Next came a thud against my ribs as he sunk his knee into me, and a glancing heel burn on my neck from Eddie. The circle shrank in around me. From the corner of my eye, moist and dripping, I saw Gody, Rita and Patty inch closer. Frankie stayed back. Suddenly, I felt a foot press down on my hand. It sprung alive with needles, and jerking my chin sideways, I saw Rita, her mouth scrunched tight, grinding her heel into my hand.

From then on, I only remember a storm of cuffs and chops and kicks hitting me as I thrashed under Mondo's grip. He crunched his knee against my head, scraping my eyebrow against the oil-crudded dirt. I tried twisting my body around to get up, yet for every strain, Mondo pressed harder, shifting the weight of his knees to counter my thrusts.

I could smell the acidy stink of the dirt, but strangely enough, there was no fear. Nor could I feel the blows, which felt like instead of me, they were hitting a slab of meat on a table. In my mind I kept saying, *Okay, you bastards, go ahead. Go ahead! See where it gets you!*

I knew that this had to be about the stupidest thing I could think about at the time, but somewhere in the back of my mind I had a thought that, once whatever it was I was being tested for came out, I'd get to go to the back room, where a couch lay against the wall and there I'd kiss Rita, or Patty, just like Frankie had promised— finally, I would hug a girl full in my arms, smell the mustiness of her breath brooding deep inside my nose, feel her lips smashing, like a kick against my mouth.

When they finally let me up, I sat there for the longest time dabbing my lips, swelling fast, flaring alive with throbs. There was also a bruise on my hand, trimmed black around the edges. My muscles felt weak, like mush, and all over my body, my bones echoed little pinpoints of pain.

I was squinching my eyes, trying to squeeze every last shudder of hurt and trembling away, when I heard Patty laughing behind me. She had a snappy laugh, like she expected everybody to crack a rib alongside her.

"Ahh, quit worrying about your lip!" Eddie scolded.

"Shut up, Eddie!" Frankie said, flicking dirt off my hair. "You'll be okay," he said, soothingly. He put his arm around my shoulders. "You'll be okay."

■ 11 ■

Going Home

The next day I woke up still bruised, but got dressed quick, feeling in my muscles a satisfying ache, like I'd done something really dangerous and survived it. We were going to hang around uptown, under the maple trees near Long's Drugstore. The guys figured we could steal some flashlight batteries, bottles of lotion or aspirin and then sell them to people looking for a bargain. While I was thinking about it, I remembered that I promised my mother I'd clean my room and rake the yard. Usually, my shoulders got slippery when my mother's hand came asking to do chores. Mops, brooms, sometimes dishes popped mysteriously out of my hands. But I was trying to help more around the house, and I was anxious to go out with the gang and didn't want Mom's eyes to narrow suspiciously.

I swept the floor of my room. I stuffed my dirty clothes in the closet, and fighting against whirlwinds from a coming storm, raked the leaves in the yard. After I was done, I rushed into the bathroom to wash up.

A feather was tickling the back of my throat. I stared into the mirror, imagining myself a brown Cary Grant and thinking about Rita, about how the night before she fluttered her eyelashes against my cheek, and stabbed the inside of my ear with the moist tip of her tongue. When she dropped hints that there'd be more surprises to come, my lungs became heavy as soaked towels.

The lightbulb in the bathroom was blazing a white star in the mirror, and looking at it, I was surprised by how much pleasure and agony could burst from one's heart at the same time. For once, I understood what my grandma used to say about happiness. She'd say that it came from breathing air that escaped from a tiny hole in heaven. But if you breathed too much of it, you became sick with the desire to go there, and you couldn't live your life properly.

At the door, I remembered my mom and yelled to her that I was going to play baseball. She was in the kitchen shifting cans around in the storage pantry. She shouted back that I should stay home since she was making chicken soup for lunch, and later planned to go with Dad to negotiate something about Grandma's house.

I picked up my old baseball mitt. I'd sort of lost the magic for baseball, and it showed in my old glove. The seams along the heel were bursting and the boot-string webbings were loose. The few times I did play, fastballs kept squirting out and popping me in the face. I knew it'd serve as a good excuse for going out, though.

I went down the hall, past Magda's room. She was in front of her old beaten-up dresser, combing her hair. She hadn't teased it yet, and her hair was a smooth current of dark, moonless water. When she saw me in the reflection of the mirror, she frowned and clacked the brush down. "What are you looking at?"

"Nothing."

She picked her brush back up and held it poised in front of the mirror. "What do you think if I peroxide my hair?" she asked, gently plucking at her eyebrow.

"You'll look like Conchita Rodriguez."

"She's a monster!"

"Well, that's how you'd look."

"Who asked you anyway," Magda said, straightening her face in the mirror.

As I went back into the kitchen I heard the electricity in the refrigerator click on. Chicken soup was bubbling on the stove, its aroma roaming like a spirit throughout the room. I found Mom inside the pantry and waved the baseball mitt in her face. "Mom, this is an important game."

"They're all important games, *mijo*," she said, putting her cleaning rag down. I followed her around the kitchen as she busied over finding a can opener. She fussed with her hair, unknotting the tangles. "What I need is a hairbrush, not a can opener."

"But, Mom, this is different. Really."

"You're going to play baseball in this weather?" She peered outside the window. The wind was splashing hard on the maple trees. "You quit playing baseball months ago, Manuel. I know that. Don't try to fool me. Besides, you came home pretty late last night."

She stopped plucking at her hair and sized me up and down. I guess my face was bruised in spots. I had put on a cotton sweatshirt and a baseball cap with the word BASEBALL knitted in big red letters on the top. I lowered the brim so that she couldn't see all that much, turned and unpinched the glove from under my arm and began smacking my fist inside it. It made a dry, hollow sound.

"Well, I *suppose* it's okay," she said, finally. "But don't come back late."

I knew she believed me about as far as she could throw the refrigerator, but I guess she was sort of surprised I even tried to *make* an excuse. Nardo wouldn't have even bothered. She'd made up her mind to leave him alone and hope for the best. I thought at first she was wishing the same for me, but the way she looked at me was different, like she knew I'd do the right thing.

After tossing my glove and baseball cap in some bushes, I ran to Long's Drugstore. It was far away, and I had to walk sometimes, and when I did I noticed how furious the wind was getting. A storm was darkening the clouds. Telephone wires whirred and papers scorched across the sidewalk. When caught in the bushes, they scrabbled noisily around like castanets before shooting out again stiff as shotgun blasts.

The guys were sitting on the stone bench when I finally got there, except Mondo, who had his hands shoved in his pockets and was leaning against the wind. Even though it was cold, he had his shirttail out, but over it he wore a dark-blue industrial jacket, unzipped. He watched a woman scramble to her car, her knees bent low and arms crossed to pin down her skirt, and cackled so loud the woman turned and scowled at him.

There was this black guy selling newspapers in front of the store. He had on a gray knit cap curled around his ears and a letterman jacket with the collar turned up. He never said anything when customers snatched a paper and rudely dished a coin at him. Then he caught Eddie eyeing him and moved over by the department store further down the mall.

Gody, wearing only a sweatshirt, kept rubbing his hands and burring his lips. His voice came with a clatter of teeth. "Maybe we shhould snatch some old lady's purse," he said, hunching over. "We'rre bound to make twenty, maaaybe thirty dollars."

Mondo smoothed back his wind-mussed hair and thought about Gody's plan. "It's true," he said. "Old white ladies sure have a *chorro* of money. Besides, their arms are so weak they almost break off when you grab their purse." He imitated an old lady trying to get her joints moving, and we laughed. Finally, he said, "Naah, ladies with money don't shop around here. They hang more around the white side of town."

"What about the newspaper guy?" Eddie suggested. "I can catch 'em."

"Naah," Mondo stressed again, this time a little less nasty. He didn't want to spoil anybody's ideas.

By then the wind was like icy fish nibbling around our pant legs. Frankie and Gody sparked a match feud, but they got more interested in watching the match suddenly puff out and flit sideways. Frankie suggested we sneak in to see the new horror movie at the Azteca Theater. Mondo squelched that with another prolonged Naaah. I didn't suggest anything.

The parking lot was almost empty. People weren't staying long to shop, but rushed around anxious to get back home. Eddie suggested again that we nab the newspaper guy before he got too far. Last time we looked, he had distanced himself from us a good half block. "Come on, you cowards," Eddie coaxed.

"Where is he then?" Mondo asked, pretending interest. We all turned around, but the guy was gone. "Well," he said, looking around, "I'm going home. Besides, there's not enough people in the store for us to steal anything without getting noticed."

As he was shaking the cold out of his legs, a huge gust of wind came splashing against the tree above us, heaving over a branch and knocking it against one of the electric wires. "That's not good," Mondo said, nodding ominously at the tree. Then, without saying good-bye, he stretched his arms, made a military salute and walked across the parking lot.

Frankie, Gody and I offered to tag along with him, but he waved us off, saying he and Patty planned to watch television, alone.

As Mondo walked across the parking lot, some old geezer came out of the store fiddling with his car keys. When he reached for the door Mondo came up behind him and twirled a fist over his bald head. Eddie moved forward, but Mondo walked quickly away, massaging and winding his arm as if he was only kidding.

"Gee, I thought he wanted to jump that guy," Eddie said glumly, walking back to us. He looked over at Mondo, edging into the wind before disappearing behind a corner building. "I guess he's too chicken, like some people I know." He upped his chin toward us.

"Yeah, but he's got a girl," Gody said, clacking his teeth.

"I got a girl, too," Eddie said, but before he could say anything more, another huge wind set off what sounded like a catapult in the tree above us. We all jerked up thinking we'd be crushed by a collapsing branch, or struck dead by a sparking power line. Instead, the whole tree jolted, as if pulled suddenly from above by the fist of a cloud. The tree snapped back cracking and groaning against the power lines.

"Heeyyy, we better get outta here," Frankie said. "Sometimes these frickin' trees kill people!"

That's when Eddie, his hand like a shovel, stopped me and said that I should stay with him.

"What're you going to do?" Frankie asked.

"Go down the mall."

"Go down the mall where?"

"Hey, who the hell do you think you are asking me questions, the FBI?" Eddie flipped the book of matches he had in his hand at Frankie's shoes.

"No," Frankie said, looking at the matches.

"Well, it's none of your damn *business*, okay. Me and Manny are just going to check out the *rucas*."

"There ain't no *rucas*," Frankie said. "We've just been talking for an hour about what we're gonna do, and now you want to go down the mall?"

"Well, so what?"

"Hey, look," Frankie said, opening his palm in appeal. "I jus' don't want you guys to try anything, that's all. We got to be together, you know, and plan it out."

"Gaaah," Eddie said, exaggerating Frankie's accusation. "Who the hell do you think we are? Are we gonna steal something? Do you think we're thieves or what?"

"Whatta you talking about?" Frankie asked, confused. He *knew* Eddie was a thief.

"I'm talking about you, *pendejo*! You stand there accusing us of stealing and then say what am *I* talking about."

"Well, I'm not accusing you of anything."

"Yeah you are. And if you don't watch it, you're going to find some teeth in your hand."

Frankie scraped his lower lip with his upper teeth, thinking. "You want to go with him?" he asked, shifting his eyes to me.

"Yeah, I'll go with him. What's the big deal?"

"Really?"

"Yeah, what's the big deal?" Eddie piped in.

You could tell by Frankie's face it was obviously a big deal. Frankie said Eddie liked to walk down the street and just for the kick of it punch some white guy in the mouth. He said Eddie liked to hit white guys square on the jaw, because their faces reddened with surprise. He hated white guys, especially those dressed in button sweaters, cotton pants and loafers, which was curious, since Eddie was a white guy himself. In fact, Mondo and Eddie weren't full brothers. Mondo's dad was named Montez, and he was in prison for assaulting a police officer, and Eddie's dad was named Owens, and he died a long time ago, knifed by a man who said he cheated at cards. But even without the splitting of names, anybody could tell they weren't all of the same blood. Mondo had curly black hair, thick enough to bend combs, and sprinkles of pimples on his cheeks and forehead. Eddie was so white, when he got agitated, little rosebuds bloomed on his face, then closed again like tiny fists.

I wished I had remembered all this when I agreed to go with Eddie, but I followed him anyway, snatching glances at Frankie and hoping maybe he'd wave me back. Instead, Frankie walked across the parking lot as if to go home, shading his eyes from blusters of dusty wind.

"What are you looking at?" Eddie asked.

"Frankie."

"Screw him! He don't make the rules." Eddie was walking fast, still angry. An empty soda can came hammering down the mall, and Eddie, with a sneer kicked it back into the shifting wind.

The day sure was wild and blustery. Trees were creaking and whining like rusty wheels, a few shreds of sunlight twisted in the branches. Shadows grew and slipped around under the trees like dolphins frolicking about, and more than once when I glanced to the side I had the feeling that a tree was walking alongside me.

Eddie didn't seem to feel the trees at all. He walked with a heavy purpose to his heels, swiveling his head, his eyes making popping noises when he blinked. Not much other than the weather was happening in the mall. A knot of cars tried to untangle at an intersection. A flying pigeon was swept crazily away by a sudden burst of wind.

Then I heard a little buffeting sound on the trees like a whole audience of people were tapping their fingers lightly on paper. I checked with my open palm and a cold needle of rain pricked my skin. I was about to tell Eddie that maybe we ought to head for home when I saw the soft blue cords in his throat tighten. He began to move faster.

Across the street, a lady with a black dress and clear plastic raincoat came rushing out of the Guarantee Savings Bank. She had a flat black purse covering her head and was hunched against the wind. Eddie paused at the curb, eyeing the woman. He glanced both ways down the street, which I thought strange, since he usually walked across streets, practically daring cars to run over him.

The lady stopped by her car and began to root for something inside her purse. The rain was beginning to tap harder on everything. While she leaned against the door, the wind flailed her plastic raincoat, and she beat it down with her hand. Finally, she plucked out some keys and opened the door.

By then the rain was splatting hard on the asphalt and glazing the windshield, and Eddie had crossed the street, moving fast, blotches of red flaming in his cheeks and his mouth set in a mean clench. Suddenly, with his legs hinging like a jackknife, he lunged and blasted his foot against the car door. The door didn't close, but instead sprung back, stopped by the lady's hand.

She was stunned. She skitted her heel on the sleek asphalt and plopped down on her butt with a splashy thud. As she did, her purse dropped, and Eddie knelt down quickly to grab it, pushing her leg away. The lady sat there, surprised, her left ankle crooked and the white slip of her dress showing through, wet and ruffled. She didn't look so pretty as when she had first walked out of the bank, and I was surprised to feel a small trickle of excitement seep down my throat.

The lady's hand must have awoken to the pain, because she looked at it like it'd been struck by lightning. The corners of her mouth twitched, and her eyes opened, amazed. Then she burst into a sudden blubbering, but stopped right away, staring numb at Eddie as he shoveled back what spilled out of her purse. For a moment I thought she wanted to touch him. Not to grab back her purse, but to touch him to see if he was really there.

Eddie was there, all right. He rose, and seeing her outstretched hand, slapped it down like a naughty child's. Then he ran back across the street, not even bothering to scan for cars.

He rushed past me, not saying anything. His lungs were pumping for air. I called for him to wait, but he didn't even turn around. I ran after him down the mall, the wind pressing my back and legs pounding hard on the sidewalk. I was afraid I'd bust a knee joint, I was running so hard. I was too hurt and bruised from the beating the day before to catch him, though. Already, he was shrinking in the distance.

Before rounding the corner of Long's Drugstore, Eddie finally turned, and that's when I recognized him as Magda's boyfriend. The distance was the same as when I first saw him near the maple trees. That's how I knew it was him. Magda wasn't seeing him anymore, because she said she never really liked him, but only wanted somebody to be with her. I tried calling again, louder, but all that came out of my throat was a tremble of vocal cords.

In that instant of trying to call out to Eddie, everything changed. It was like I'd finally seen my own face and recognized myself; recognized who I really should be. Then I didn't feel like catching up to Eddie anymore. Instead, I wanted to grab him, and scold him about how to treat people, how to be somebody who knows how to treat people: like my sister; like that lady. But I didn't really feel like running anymore. Forget Eddie, I thought. Even if I caught him, he wouldn't understand anything I'd say. I slowed down to a walk just as the wind and rain were dying.

I stopped at the parking lot and halfheartedly searched around. It was empty of cars. Puddles of rain mirrored a hundred cloudy skies. Eddie was nowhere to be seen. The newspaper guy had migrated back to his spot in front of the drugstore, although he was packing his things. Some newspapers, soggy in his hand, were bleeding ink between his knuckles. He tossed them into a trash can, wrung the ink from his fingers and gazed at me with pitying eyes.

A thought rushed through my mind that maybe he had seen what had happened, but I figured it happened too far away.

"Where did he go?" I asked.

The guy shifted his eyes across the street, the same corner where Mondo, Frankie and Gody had gone. He flicked more ink off his fingers and hunched over his bag as if crouching over a fire. I shrugged and rubbed my forehead with the back of my hand.

Suddenly, the guy's head lifted and eyes focused over my shoulder. Down the mall, over by the department store, a black-and-white cop car came cruising in and out of the line of trees. Two cops were inside, and the passenger one pointed his finger at me and shouted to the driver. The driver pressed down the pedal and the car jerked forward, wobbling as it climbed over a curb.

I was about to bolt down the street, but the newspaper guy stopped me, saying, "Hey man. Just cool it."

The cops were on us instantly, swerving to a stop. My neck was hot as radiation and my brain racing for excuses. A sponge was in my throat and I was afraid that if I tried to talk, instead of words, a sob would squeeze out. What surprised me, though, was that the cops were not getting out of the car. I thought for sure they'd wrestle the handcuffs on me in a second.

The passenger cop, a blueberry-faced guy with a swollen, boozer's nose, and a glassy look on his face, started banging on the side door with his palm. "Hey you! Kid! Were you the one chasing that guy who stole the lady's purse?"

Before I could answer, the black guy shouted across my ear. "Yeah officer, he's the one. He came chasing that guy through the mall."

"Which way did he go?"

"He don't know, officer. He come over here to ask me, and I says I just seen him run around that corner over there not two minutes ago." He raised a finger in the direction Eddie had gone, and the car, as if pushed by the magic of his pointed finger, lurched backward, cranked into gear and gunned across the parking lot, spraying through the puddles.

As the cop car swung and squealed around the corner, the guy with the newspapers hurried to finish packing. In the trees, a silky rain was again falling with long, gathering sighs.

After packing his stuff, the guy turned to me and this time without a smile, said, "I know. I know you was with him. But they don't have to know everything. Let them deal with their own kind as they see fit." He left among coughs so ratchety you'd think he was dying of double pneumonia.

I began to walk home. The rain had died, but trash started crawling across the sidewalk again. As I neared our projects, I watched the branches of the elm trees creaking sluggishly back and forth. I stopped once to listen to some leaves falling. They'd *tap tap tap* on the branches before hitting the sidewalk, then a toss of wind would fling them in the air.

When I neared the Garcias' house, I saw them

on their front porch, bundled up in coats, eating apples. I was surprised that a prickle of fear didn't rise behind my neck. Instead I felt numb, except that it was a glowing sort of numbness pushing out from me in slow, easy pulses.

Stinky, a saltshaker pinched under his forearm, was trying to pry open a green apple with his thumbs. When he couldn't, he licked it, sprinkled some salt on the moisture and crunched a bite, squeezing his face away from the tartness. Noticing me, he stared at me a while, as if he'd noticed something he'd never, in all the years he'd known me, seen. Then he winked and gestured to me if I wanted some of his apple. I waved my hand no, and he began unclogging the holes of the saltshaker.

When I opened the door to our house, the sun, out again, came rushing into the living room. Shadows lifted from the floor like a flock of birds rising into the horizon, and light guttered through the room, slapping away the dark for good. A huge splash of light even bounced off the glass-top coffee table and raked my eyes; a snake of it slithered on the painting of the Last Supper. So much brightness made me realize how tired my eyes were, and I wobbled into the room on soft legs.

Magda and Pedi were lying asleep, on opposite sides of the couch, each crunching their end of the blanket against their chest. Magda's hair was fanned out on a pillow, unteased. I watched her as she lay there, her mouth half open, a thin line of black mascara leaking from the corner of one eye. I went over and wiped it, and she snuffled and turned her face away.

Then I sat down on Dad's cushioned chair and watched them. I won't say why, because there's no way of explaining why, even if I could or wanted to, but I knew, as my eyes got drowsy and the bright walls of the room glowed around me, that I'd never again see anything so wondrous as my two sisters lying on the couch. And it wasn't just them, but the whole room: the squiggly TV, the lumpy cherub angels on the frame of the painting, the glass-top coffee table, my mother's animals, gleaming in the sunlight. This room was what my mother spent so much energy cleaning and keeping together, and what my father spent so much energy tearing apart. And it was wondrous, like a place I was meant to be. A place, I felt, that I had come back to after a long journey of being away. My home. The light in the room was closing in around me,

I was so sleepy. It was dissolving and sifting in through my eyelashes in thin, filtered streams, and then there was only the dull blood under my eyelids, then dark, then sleep.